Charlotte

&

MR. ABERNATHY

KD McCrite

Text copyright © 2022 by McCrite, KD
All Rights Reserved. Printed in the United States of America

Published by Motina Books, LLC, Van Alstyne, Texas
www.MotinaBooks.com

Library of Congress Cataloguing-in-Publication Data:

Names: McCrite, KD
Title: Charlotte & Mr. Abernathy
Description: First Edition. | Van Alstyne: Motina Books, 2022
Identifiers:

LCCN: 2021949474

Lexile Measure: 570L

ISBN-13: 978-1-945060-37-3 (paperback)
ISBN-13: 978-1-945060-39-7 (e-book)
ISBN-13: 978-1-945060-38-0 (hardcover)

Subjects: BISAC:

JUVENILE FICTION / Ghost Stories

Cover Design: Venessa Cerasale
Interior Design: Diane Windsor

Other Works by KD McCrite

The Confessions of April Grace Series (Middle-Grade)

In Front of God and Everybody

Cliques, Hicks, and Ugly Sticks

Chocolate-Covered Baloney

Cozy Mysteries

Deed in the Attic

Unfinished Symphony

Stony Point Christmas

The Ring in the Attic

Raven Threads

Double Strand Deception

Unraveled Stalkings

A Dark Turnover

Sweet Sabotage

Honey-Dipped Secrets

Broken Melody

Book Clubbed

Trifling with Trouble

A Lost Clause

A Scary Tale Wedding

Dedicated to Linda Knight.
Best friends are forever.

CHAPTER ONE

The first morning after Charlotte Franklin and her mom moved into the ugly yellow house on Timberline Avenue, Charlotte found a stranger sitting at the kitchen table. The kitchen was chilly, as if someone had left the refrigerator door open too long. She stopped dead in her tracks, not moving, not even breathing.

Charlotte had been hearing the sound of wind chimes again, so maybe she should have expected to see someone, somewhere, in that house. Every time she'd noticed the soft, tinkling music while she and Mom were moving or cleaning, she'd tried to ignore it. She had told herself the wind chimes were probably hanging on a neighbor's front porch, and the breeze carried the sound into the house through the open windows. She didn't really believe it, though. She knew what the sound of chimes meant.

The moment she saw the strange man in the kitchen,

the wind chimes fell silent.

His looks made her think of a cantaloupe. He had a nearly-bald head with a round face, and his round eyes blinked at her from behind small round glasses. His mustache was curled at the ends in nearly perfect circles. The longer he and Charlotte stared at each other, the bigger and rounder his eyes grew.

Charlotte knew Mom would be unable to hear her yell above the sound of running water in the upstairs shower. She also knew if she ran from the room, he'd follow her.

She was not a screaming, crying, fainting kind of girl. She always took action, even when she was pretty sure it was doomed to failure.

Gulping back her fear, she grabbed Mom's heavy white-marble rolling pin. One hard thump on the head from that thing could knock out a normal man. She hoped he was a normal man. A real one. She shook the rolling pin at him.

"You better leave right now." She spoke so forcefully no one would guess she shivered like a wet dog inside her skin.

He leaned forward, still gawking as if he'd never seen a lanky twelve-year-old girl with long blonde hair.

"Are you speaking to me?" His voice was precise and clipped, with a strange accent.

"We're the only ones in this room, so yeah, I'm talking to you."

The man at the table raised one pudgy hand, thumb

2

tucked against his palm. "How many fingers am I holding up?"

"What? Four! You need to leave, right now."

"Four! Yes!" He stretched both arms upward and gazed at the ceiling. "Thank the bright stars!" He lowered his arms and looked at her. "Have you the least notion how long it has been since anyone has seen me?"

Charlotte's arm began to ache from holding the heavy rolling pin aloft.

"Are you gonna sit there and talk weird, or am I gonna have to do something?"

He waved one hand. "Go ahead and crack my skull, child. It has been cracked before by someone with murderous intent." His gaze bored into her. "I can't believe after all the people who have lived here, someone finally sees me. And wouldn't you know it would be a little girl who brandishes a pastry roller with ease!"

"I'm not a little girl!" She raised the rolling pin a little higher and glowered at him. "The Park City Police Department's motto is We're Only a Phone Call Away."

The man sighed, and a slight chilly breeze blew through the kitchen. He pointed at the big white stove. It was as old as everything else in the house, but it gleamed brightly from the scrubbing Mom had given it before they moved in. Charlotte had polished the chrome trim until it shone like mirrors.

"I've had many a fine breakfast prepared on that stove," he said. "Two pieces of crisp bacon, an egg poached to perfection, three slices of rye toast with strawberry preserves, a tall glass of milk, and a bracing cup of coffee. Every morning without fail." He sighed again. Another chill stirred. "I miss breakfasts."

"Then go home and make yourself some. Or go to the police station and turn yourself in. They'll feed you in jail."

He turned a sorrowful gaze to her. "Dear child, you fail to understand. I am home. I built this house and lived in it for twenty-eight years."

She closed her ears to those words in the same way she'd closed her ears to the warning tones of wind chimes.

The one cell phone in the house was upstairs, so with the rolling pin still firmly in her right hand, Charlotte marched to the black phone hanging on the wall. It was so old she doubted it worked. She lifted the receiver. A dial tone hummed dully in her ear. She called 9-1-1.

"I wish the police *could* help," the man said. "I have a feeling there is somewhere else I'm supposed to be."

The truth shivered across Charlotte's mind, but she refused to think about it. Maybe, just maybe he was a real man.

The 9-1-1 operator came on the line. Charlotte gave her name and information, answering all the operator's questions.

"He's just sitting here at the table. I told him to get out or I was gonna call the cops. Yes, ma'am, I under-stand. Okay. I will."

She shot a look at the man who merely stared back. The corners of his mouth drooped like limp spaghetti.

The sound of the shower finally stopped. She yelled as loud as she could. "Mom! There's a man in our kitchen!"

Her mother rushed downstairs, her short blond hair sticking up in wet spikes all over her head. Her bare feet left damp footprints behind her. Mom was an anxious woman who startled easily. Sudden loud noises especially upset her. She tightened the belt on her robe and stared at Charlotte with fear on her face.

"What's wrong? Are you hurt or—"

She broke off as Charlotte handed her the telephone and pointed to the man at the table.

"They want to talk to you ... about him."

Looking mystified and still worried, Mom took the receiver. As she talked, she fingered the little gold circlet necklace she wore. Dad had given it to her on the day Charlotte was born, and she never took it off.

"Hello? This is Jennifer Franklin. What's this about?"

The entire time Mom talked with the 9-1-1 operator, Charlotte stood, arm outstretched, index finger pointing at the man at the table. She still held the rolling pin.

Mom hung up the phone. "Give me that rolling pin before you drop it on your foot." Her voice was strained. Charlotte handed it over.

"Mom, don't you see him? Right there at the table, in the chair closest to the window?" If only her pleading could convince Mom....

"I told you so," the man said in a sorrowful voice.

5

Her mother put the rolling pin back in its place. She rubbed both arms as if she were cold.

"Honey, no one is sitting at the table." She heaved a deep sigh as she turned away and began making her morning coffee. "Please don't start this again."

"Start what again?" But she knew.

"That Janelle Dunmark business."

"Mom! I was a little kid then." She wished she could forget about Janelle Dunmark. She wished she could no longer hear those stupid chimes at odd times or see the others she didn't want to see—those people no one else could see.

Mom closed her eyes. "Just … don't start. Okay?"

Charlotte hadn't cried since they left her dad in Macomb last month. Even then she had swallowed back the lump in her throat and squeezed her eyelids shut so tight no tears could escape. Now two hot, fat tears dribbled down her cheeks.

When a police officer came to the house just a few minutes later, Mom tried to explain her daughter's call to emergency services.

"She has such an active imagination," she concluded. "You know how kids are."

The officer eyed Charlotte steadily.

"You're old enough to know better," he said quietly. "Someone with a *real* problem might need me right now, and I'm not there to help them."

She wished she could shrivel up, completely out of his sight. There was no way he'd believe the truth, so she murmured, "I'm sorry, sir."

He looked at her a bit longer then turned to Mom. "As a mother, it's your responsibility to keep your child from potentially harmful behavior. If she makes another phony emergency call, I'm afraid she won't be the only one in trouble."

He shifted his gaze from one to the other, told them to have a nice day, then he turned and went to his patrol car. They watched him drive away. Mom drew in a deep breath and blew it out slowly.

"I have to get back to work now." She walked to the door leading upstairs. "If you ever pull this stunt again, you will be in trouble like never before. As it is, you're grounded from the party this weekend."

Charlotte's stomach hurt as if she'd swallowed rocks.

"You mean I can't go to Olivia's birthday party?"

Her mom went up the stairs. "That's what I mean."

"But I haven't seen Olivia since … ." Since the last day of school, she ended silently.

"You should have thought of that before pulling a foolish prank." Mom paused at the top of the steps. "As soon as you're dressed, please bring in the newspaper."

"May I at least text her?"

"No, you may not. I'll let her know you won't be there."

"Mooooom!"

She closed the door to her design studio, obviously focused once more on "moving forward" with her career.

She was *always* focused on moving forward with her career. At least that's what she told Dad the night Charlotte overheard them talking about separating.

Why couldn't she 'move forward' back home instead of dragging them to this horrible place so far from Charlotte's dad?

Outside, the newspaper was next to a scraggly old bush close to the front porch steps. That bush looked like it felt as bad as Charlotte. All it needed was water and some pruning. Lucky old bush. All the water in the world wouldn't help Charlotte.

A boy in the yard of the little white house across the street came to the edge of the sidewalk and called out to her, "Hey there!"

The morning's events had upset her so much that she barely lifted a hand to acknowledge him. She stomped back into the kitchen and slammed the newspaper down on the table.

She leaned forward and looked right into the clear blue eyes of the round-faced man.

"Just because of you, I'm *grounded* from my best friend's party and sleepover. And all my friends live clear over in Macomb! Dad will probably have to work most of the weekend, so I won't get to see him, either. Thank you very much."

The man at the table shrugged both droopy shoulders and let out a long, mournful sigh. The dingy curtains stirred in a cool draft.

"It is not *my* fault you are the only one who can see

me," he said. "I have waited for almost a century for someone, *anyone*, to notice me."

Mom had always believed Janelle Dunmark was nothing more than a figment of Charlotte's imagination. She supposed the pranks, the missing items, the broken or misplaced knickknacks were something Charlotte had done. No matter how often Charlotte tried to explain, Mom refused to listen. Now here was someone else causing trouble and she was taking the blame. She'd just ignore him from now until the end of time.

She huffed loudly, stalked to the cabinet, and got out a box of Corn Flakes. She fixed her cereal and sat down, wishing she could eat in her room, away from the round blue eyes that watched her so carefully. But Mom had a strict rule about eating only in the kitchen.

The aroma of fresh coffee filled the air. The man lifted his face and drew in a deep breath. "Ah, I love the smell of morning coffee."

She said nothing.

"It's bracing! Invigorating!"

She kept silent.

"I used to eat Corn Flakes," he sighed, watching her.

She forgot her resolve to ignore him. "I thought you ate eggs and bacon and rye toast."

"I did. But I liked Corn Flakes as a midnight snack. Helped me to sleep."

Charlotte slurped milk from her cereal bowl and didn't reply. She figured he frowned at her slurping. Maybe he missed slurping, as well as eating and drinking.

"You and your mother have really cleaned this kitchen. You've done a fine job."

She'd been taught to be polite. Because he'd noticed how hard they'd worked to make the old house clean and livable, the polite thing to do was respond.

"Yeah, well, this whole house was way more disgusting than it is now. My mom and I spent two whole weeks cleaning it before she would allow us to sleep even one night in here."

"Yes, I know. I watched the two of you work. And your mother was right: you should never live or sleep in chaos and filth. The last tenants were terrible housekeepers."

She slid her eyes sideways to look at him. "They were total slobs. I found half a loaf of moldy bread in my bedroom closet."

He leaned forward. "And did you notice the bucket with the rancid mop next to the back door?"

They both looked at where the bucket used to be before Mom had carted the nasty thing outside to the trash.

"That mop made me gag." She got up and washed out her bowl.

"If I could have gagged, I would have done so."

Charlotte put her bowl away. She turned to him and rested both hands on her hips. "Who are you, anyway?"

He stared at her from behind the round glasses. "My dear child, who and what do you suppose I am?"

"Maybe you're someone I made up in my imagination."

He smiled the sad smile that was beginning to look familiar.

"No, my dear, you may rest assured I am not imaginary. My name is Clarence Albert Abernathy. I built this house in 1901, and I was murdered right here in this very kitchen on the twentieth day of May 1929."

CHAPTER TWO

"Well, upon my word," Clarence Albert Abernathy said, after a moment or two. "You're very calm facing the ghost of a murdered person."

What had he expected Charlotte to do? Scream? Faint? Go running from the room in a panic? That was not Charlotte Franklin's way of handling situations. She was a little scared, but only because she didn't know what this ghost wanted from her. More than that, she was curious.

Her dad was a detective. She'd often overheard him talking to Mom about his work or talking on the phone to other detectives. She wanted to work in the field of investigation someday, so she usually asked him a lot of questions about his job.

"You were *murdered?*" she now asked Mr. Abernathy.

"I believe so, yes." He pointed to a place near the stove. "I was found right there, lying in a pool of blood, my head bashed in."

She looked down, half-expecting to see ghost blood.

"Ew. Who killed you?"

"I don't know. I had many acquaintances but few friends—I was so busy, you know—but never realized I had an actual enemy."

The little stirring in her chest made Charlotte feel soft and sad and helpless. She disliked that feeling.

"If I knew who took my life and why," he continued, "I believe I could finally rest in peace."

"You mean you might 'move on'?"

"Exactly. I would hope so."

Charlotte pondered this for a little bit. "Do you think the local newspaper would have had a story about your murder?"

"Oh, surely. After all, I helped to found the Bank of Park City, and I was the vice president of the loan department. I was an important person in this town." He sat up straighter than ever and smoothed the lapels of his jacket. He certainly looked like he might have been an important citizen all those years ago.

She thought about this situation some more. "And in all these years no one in this house saw you, ever?" she asked.

"As I said before, you are the first. Oh, there was a time or two when I thought someone *might* have noticed me, but they chose to ignore me."

Charlotte narrowed her eyes to slits, trying to see if

any part of him was invisible, but he looked pretty solid to her.

"That's about the saddest thing ever. Mom and I were here every day cleaning this creepy old dump, but today is the first time I saw you."

Mr. Abernathy gave her a haughty look and yanked on the cuffs of his sleeves. "I do not appreciate having my home referred to as a 'creepy old dump.'"

"Listen. This place is drafty and creaky and smelly...with a ghost in it. That makes it creepy. Ask anyone."

"That's an unpleasant attitude."

"Having a ghost at the kitchen table who gets me in trouble is worse. If you'd just shown yourself to my mom, I wouldn't be grounded from Olivia's sleepover this weekend."

An awful tickle choked the back of her throat. She reminded herself she was not a crier. Or a whiner.

"Young woman," Mr. Abernathy said in a stern tone, "do you believe I chose not to attract the attention of others? Do you assume I enjoy sitting here, unseen, unheard, my legacy forgotten?"

"I bet if you really wanted someone to see you, they would! You probably never tried hard enough."

He blew out a huffy, cold breath and glared at her.

"You haven't the faintest notion what it is like to be unseen," he said.

"Oh, excuse me! Sometimes I might as well be a ghost."

15

He sat back, slumping a little in the chair. "You think people don't see you? *You* are not a ghost, child."

She waved an impatient hand. "They see me, but they don't listen to me. If they did, we'd still be living with my dad in our nice new house and not in this awful old wreck."

He frowned, and it made his plump round face sink in a little, like a deflated balloon.

She took a glass out of the cabinet. The old cupboard door, warped and dingy, refused to shut completely. She pushed it several times, but it sagged open again.

"See?" She pointed to the offending door. "Back home our cabinets are nice and even, and all the doors shut. And our kitchen is the color of cream, not this Pepto-Bismol pink."

She poured orange juice into her glass.

"This was once the most beautiful kitchen of any house on this street." Pride beamed out of Mr. Abernathy like the glow from a new flashlight. "In fact, this was the most beautiful house on the entire block."

"Yeah, right." Charlotte sipped her juice.

"There are photographs to prove it!"

She all but rolled her eyes. She didn't care if the house was once Buckingham Palace. Right then it was old and ugly. In a few months, winter would arrive, and they'd be chattering with cold. Just last week Mom said they'd probably have to stuff rags in the cracks to keep the wind out. She had said it cheerfully, as if the thought of living in a drafty old house stuffed with rags would be more fun than Disneyland.

"I would show those photographs to you, if I could," he continued, "but I doubt I can make it to the attic room."

"We hauled a bunch of leftover junk into the attic so my mom could have most of the upstairs for her workspace. If there had been any pictures up there, we'd have found 'em while we cleaned. And we didn't."

"I promise you, they are there."

"Uh huh. If that's so, then go get them. And while you're upstairs, show yourself to my mom. Tell her she should let me go to the party after all, since I didn't lie about you!"

The two of them glared at each other, Charlotte daring him to prove his claim, Mr. Abernathy's expression as reproachful as a stern schoolteacher.

"All right." He stood. As round and squat as the Pillsbury Doughboy, he wore a striped, gray suit with a vest and a white shirt. He straightened his red bow tie and buttoned his jacket. He looked nervous, as if he were about to make a speech in front of a lot of people.

"Don't be afraid, Mr. Abernathy."

"I'm not afraid. I'm simply gathering my strength." He closed his eyes and sucked in a deep breath.

Charlotte never realized ghosts could take deep breaths like that.

"Go on when you're ready," she said. "But don't scare Mom by jumping out at her, or anything. When she's involved in her work, it's like she's asleep even

17

though she's awake. You have to be gentle."

"She won't see me," he insisted. Then he bowed slightly from the waist and gestured toward the door. "Ladies first."

She led the way out of the kitchen and up the steep, narrow staircase. At the top of the steps, she glanced back.

Mr. Abernathy was halfway up the staircase and fading fast.

"I told you so…." he said, and then he was gone.

CHAPTER

THREE

"**M**r. Abernathy!" Charlotte yelped.

She stared at the empty space where the man had been a moment earlier.

"Charlotte?" Mom came out of her sewing studio, a red drafting pencil in one hand and a bright yellow measuring tape dangling from her neck like a skinny scarf. She wore a dazed, half-panicked expression. Charlotte learned long ago when Mom looked like that, no one should bother her unless the house was on fire, or someone was injured or violently ill.

"He just…faded away," Charlotte choked out.

"Huh? What?"

Charlotte already was grounded for the weekend; she didn't want to be grounded for a month. She dared not explain. Instead, she tried to soothe Mom.

"Nothing," she said. "A little accident on the stairs. Sorry."

Her mom stared at her with that faraway look on her face.

"Shall I bring you some coffee?" Charlotte asked.

"Thanks, honey." She went back into her room. Her blood was probably half-coffee by now, the way she drank it all day.

Mr. Abernathy was sitting at the table when Charlotte walked into the kitchen.

"You see?" he said, spreading his hands. "I can't move from place to place in the house without ... withering."

"Well, you do look sort of sick for a dead person," Charlotte said. "Are you supposed to be that color?"

He looked down at himself. "What color?"

"Pasty pink and a little yellow."

"Charlotte?" Mom called from upstairs. "Honey, did you say you'd bring me some coffee?"

"Yes, ma'am." Charlotte filled a cup. "I suppose ghosts don't drink coffee, do they?"

Mr. Abernathy offered up one of his sighs. "No. Nor can we eat pie. I miss pie."

"If you keep sighing that way, you'll freeze everything in this kitchen. You're better than a refrigerator, you know that?"

Upstairs, Charlotte handed Mom a large cup full of steaming coffee. She watched her sketch and measure, and then work with numbers on the computer, making a new pattern. Charlotte wondered if there was anything more boring than designing clothes, especially as doing

21

so involved math. She was a smart girl, but math got on her nerves.

Mr. Abernathy had been a banker. He was probably good with numbers. He probably loved math problems. But still. Being a math-loving ghost stuck in the kitchen had to be terrible. She wished she knew how to help him.

At this point he no longer frightened her, especially as it seemed all he could do was sigh and look sad. If she were trapped in that old kitchen, would she feel sorry for herself and sigh all the time? She most certainly would *not*. She'd figure out a way to be seen and heard, and she'd get out of that place.

"Mom," she said softly, "may I talk to you?"

"Hmmm?" Mom was so lost in thoughts of her newest design that an entire hip-hop band could be singing and dancing in her studio, and she wouldn't hear or see them.

"Never mind."

Charlotte figured she felt more invisible than Mr. Abernathy ever had. At least *his* mother never ignored him in favor of her work. Or maybe she had. At any rate, she needed to figure out what to do about that dead man in the kitchen.

She went to her room at the end of the hall to think about things.

That old house was big, but a twin-sized bed, small table, and small chest filled her bedroom. She ended up keeping her shorts and t-shirts in a plastic laundry basket because her closet was so tiny. The ugly beige walls depressed her. At least her familiar quilt and big fluffy pillow made the room feel a little bit familiar.

She flopped, tummy-down, on the bed and propped her chin on her hands. Gazing outside through the tall narrow window, she watched sunlight dance in the upper branches of a big magnolia tree. The thick, waxy-petal white flowers smelled like lemons, and their fragrance was about the only thing Charlotte could think of that made her day worth a hoot.

She had lived her entire life in Macomb. A few months ago, she and her parents moved from their townhouse to a brand-new house in a new subdivision on the edge of town. Clean and fresh and pretty, it practically glowed with newness. Back in Macomb, Charlotte had a big bedroom and plenty of space. She had her own computer and phone, just like a normal girl.

Here in this old house, she had nothing. No tablet or laptop, no smartphone, not even a boring old cordless phone, just that awful black phone on the wall in the kitchen. Plus, there was only one electrical outlet in each room. How was she supposed to survive living in the Stone Age?

Mom had hated the new house in Macomb. She called it a cookie cutter. She'd said it had no character, and none of the rooms were "conducive to creativity." Dad reminded her it was in the best neighborhood and had the best school. He told her she could make clothes in the spare room. His words had upset her.

She'd said he knew nothing about being a designer

or even being creative, for that matter, and he'd never supported her dream, ever, and he said, yes he had, but it seemed far-fetched to him because there were too many fashion designers out there anyway, so why didn't she just keep making nice outfits for the ladies in Macomb like she'd been doing, and Mom said she wanted to create her own look not use someone else's pattern, and their arguments went on and on and on, and Charlotte thought their fighting would never end.

As soon as school let out for summer vacation, the arguments stopped. And they stopped because Mom moved herself and Charlotte away from Dad, the new house, friends, and everything familiar.

Charlotte still wondered why she and Mom had to move. When she'd asked her parents why they couldn't work out their differences, they each said the same thing: "I don't know."

Well, if they didn't know, who did? She hoped they figured it out. Soon.

She flipped over on her back and stared up at the ceiling. She'd seen so little of Park City that she didn't know if she liked it or not. It was larger than Macomb, and that meant bigger schools. Just the thought of a new school caused her stomach to clench. For the first time in her life, she'd be the new kid. All she knew about being a new kid was the awfulness she'd read about in books or seen in videos—those new kids were usually bullied and teased.

Charlotte had dealt with bullies before. They picked

on smaller kids or the quiet, studious ones. They'd tried to get Charlotte to join in the taunting and unkind tricks, but she refused. She often knew how to act like an adult, and that's how she acted toward the bullies. No nonsense, no smiles, no participation other than to stand up for the victims. The bullies learned to leave her alone.

She hoped she could make friends—good friends who would not change. In the last year, Olivia and Chloe had started acting in ways they'd never done before. They wanted to be part of the popular crowd, and that meant they treated some friends differently, weren't as nice or as friendly as they used to be. Charlotte worried they were turning into mean girls. She cared nothing about being popular, so more and more Olivia and Chloe left her out.

Charlotte never had a lot of friends, even in Macomb. Mom, who was satisfied with her designs, patterns, and sewing, hated the distraction of having other kids around. Too much chaos and noise, she said.

Not many friends in Macomb, Charlotte thought, and probably not many friends here.

The only kids she saw in this neighborhood had been a little kid on a tricycle and that scruffy-looking older boy across the street.

She figured poor ol' Mr. Abernathy felt as bad as she did.

She slid off the bed, changed out of her pajamas into pair of jeans and a white t-shirt, then brushed her hair, and went downstairs.

The dearly departed occupant of the kitchen was reading the newspaper. She stopped short and gawped at him.

"I didn't know you could do that," she said.

He looked at her over the top of the paper. "Do what? Read?"

"No, pick up the newspaper and open it."

"Well, that just proves one never knows what one's capabilities are unless one tries them."

His formal speech irritated her a little. She said, "You mean, you never know what you can do until you do it?"

"Exactly." He gazed at her thoughtfully, then turned back to the paper. "There is one certainty—politics have not changed in nearly a century. Of course, you'd know nothing about that, would you?" He raised one eyebrow. "Or would you?"

Charlotte couldn't think of anything more boring than a political discussion unless it was a discussion about algebra.

"Not really."

"In my day, some women were quite vocal about politics and voting power."

"I will be, too, probably, someday when I'm grown. But I have other things to think about now, and none of them have to do with who's running for mayor of Park City."

Mr. Abernathy shook his head and tsk-tsked between his teeth as if she'd given him backtalk. "Ah, to be young and carefree," he said. "One day you will have the responsibilities of running a home and taking care of your husband and children."

She rolled her eyes. "Whoever said being a kid is carefree? Besides, getting married and having a family doesn't sound like such a hot idea to me. Everyone is miserable."

He cleared his throat as if he thought the subject was unfit for someone her age. Charlotte was impressed a ghost could clear his throat at all.

She pulled out a chair and sat across the table from him. "Mr. Abernathy, would you like to hang out?"

"*Hang out?*" He looked and sounded horrified.

She nodded. "You know, talk about stuff. Get to know each other. Be friends."

His eyes widened. "Friends? The two of us?"

"Yeah. I mean, well, I'm stuck here and so are you. Right now, pretty much all we have is each other."

He put down the newspaper, smoothed it with the flat of both hands.

"Well," he said, slowly as if he were thinking it over, "I'm not sure a friendship is possible. You are, after all, only a little girl—"

She stiffened. "I am *not* a little girl! I'm twelve, thank you very much!"

"Ah," he said mildly. "Well, I beg your pardon. Nevertheless, I hardly see how a young lady of the 21st century and a deceased banker from 1929 could possibly have anything on which to build a friendship."

Charlotte twisted her mouth and frowned.

"You know what you are? A Debbie Downer."

"I beg your pardon?"

She sought for a term he might understand. "A party pooper. A wet blanket."

He brushed both palms over his lapels. "Oh, you mean a Gloomy Gus."

"Whatever. Why do you want to think the worst? Instead of looking at our differences, let's figure out reasons to be friends."

He blinked and said nothing.

"I bet we have plenty in common," she continued, scooting a bit forward in her chair. "For instance, you said you liked pie. I like pie, so we have that in common."

"Unfortunately, my dear," he said, all huffy, "I can no longer *enjoy* pie."

"But I can eat it, then tell you about it."

Mr. Abernathy grunted and shifted and harrumphed deep in his throat. "I hardly see how that qualifies as any type of commonality," he said, "nor would it behoove me to hear about something I can no longer enjoy."

She narrowed her eyes. "You sure use a lot of big words."

"Yes. I'm educated."

She cocked her head to one side. "You said you were murdered right here in this kitchen, right?"

He nodded. "Yes, but I know none of the particulars. Who did it, or why, or who found my body, or what was

28

done with it after it was discovered."

Charlotte tapped her right foot against the floor and gazed him with her fist curled beneath her chin. He twitched in his chair and fiddled with his bow tie.

"What are you gawping at, child?" he asked after a time. "A gimlet-eyed stare fixed upon one's elders not only is disconcerting, but it is also rude."

"I was just thinking…."

"Have I something on the end of my nose?" He dusted it with his fingertips.

"No. But when I concentrate, I have to focus on something so my thoughts don't fly around. I didn't realize I was staring at your nose."

He took off his glasses, frowned at them, and put them on again. "So what were these flying-thoughts of yours?"

"Here's the thing." She stopped foot-tapping and staring. She sat up straight. "I think we should try to find out who killed you."

CHAPTER FOUR

Mr. Abernathy shook his head and wagged one finger back and forth like a windshield wiper.

"A little girl cannot figure out how I died," he said.

She flipped one hand. "There you go, being negative. And, please, stop calling me a little girl. I don't call you a *ghoul*, do I?"

He scowled. "A ghoul is a hideous thing that feeds on corpses! I am a spirit."

"Just my point. So, please, don't call me something I'm not."

He fiddled with the buttons on his vest and his scowl faded. "I'll do my utmost to spare your sensitivities in the future. Nonetheless, I hardly see how you can solve my murder. No one else has."

"Did anyone try?"

He turned a mournful gaze out the window and sighed. "Not to my knowledge, but then how would I know? I am trapped here."

If she'd had her phone, she could've figured it out. A few taps, and she'd probably learn exactly what happened to him.

But Mom already made it clear they would have limited minutes on the phone. She also insisted that the one and only computer in the house was for her business, not Charlotte's fun. Charlotte would be allowed to use it only for schoolwork. The first day of school was weeks away. Her dad would've paid for all the minutes she could use, but Mom's dogged independence and refusal to let him provide anything other than money for food and electricity wasn't going to stop Charlotte.

"I'll find out for you." When he raised one eyebrow, she continued, "I'm going to be an investigative reporter when I'm grown."

"A reporter?" A look of distaste passed across his face.

She huffed. "What's wrong with that? You wouldn't have anything to read in the newspapers if journalists hadn't written news stories."

"Well," he said begrudgingly, "you do have a point."

"I know. And reporters dig into mysteries to find their stories and solve them. You'll be my first case." She sat back and beamed at him, fully expecting him to nod and smile. After all, solving his murder was what he'd been wanting and waiting for all these years.

He removed his glasses, blew on the lenses with a

cold breath, then put them back on and peered at her over the top of them as if he thought her appearance might have changed.

"Indeed?" He sounded so stuck-up and superior when he said this that Charlotte's hackles rose.

"Yes. Why?" She gave him a dirty look. "Don't tell me you believe girls aren't smart enough or brave enough or clever enough—"

He held up one hand in a shushing gesture.

"I perceive you are a young suffragette, so let us not quarrel. How do you propose to accomplish this objective, pray tell?"

She said nothing just to let him know he'd aggravated her. Finally, she unclenched her jaw.

"My dad is a detective in Macomb, so I've learned a few things about uncovering information and finding clues. You'll have to trust me."

"I always found that trusting others is a highly suspect activity."

Charlotte leaned toward him. "You said earlier if you found out who killed you and why they did it, maybe you could finally rest in peace."

"Yes, but I hardly see how—"

"You should trust that I can find out for you, because *I am not dumb.*"

She let her words hang between them, then sat back. His mouth formed an "O," making his face as round as a grapefruit.

"Very well, then. Proceed with your investigation. I

would shake your hand to close the deal, but…" He fluttered his pudgy fingers. "I seem only to be able to turn the pages in the newspaper."

Charlotte tried to be serious and grown up about this new venture, but excitement quivered through her insides. She jumped up from the table.

"Where are you going?" he asked.

"I'll be right back." She rushed up to her room and rummaged in her backpack for a pencil and notebook. "This would be so much easier if I could get online," she muttered as she hurried down the stairs.

Reporters didn't run when their subject sat in the other room. She paused, took in a deep breath, lifted her shoulders, and walked into the kitchen as if she was totally grown-up.

"I would offer you coffee, but…." she said to Mr. Abernathy.

"Thank you. I would happily accept it, if I could."

The air turned cold for a few seconds with his long sigh.

She settled down across from him, opened the notebook and ran her hand down the first clean page, getting it all smooth and ready for the words she'd write.

"Now," she said, picking up the pencil, "let's get to work."

"I was born February 3, 1879, and I died May 27, 1929."

"Golly. That was a long time ago!"

"Indeed." He sniffed as if this remark offended him.

"Do you want to know of my illnesses, accidents, and mishaps?"

She frowned. "Do they have anything to do with what happened on May 27, 1929?"

"No."

"Then tell me about all that later. Let's solve your mystery first."

"Very well." He folded his hands on the table and sat up straighter than ever.

"Did you have any enemies?" she asked.

"My dear child," he said with a snooty tone in his voice, "I was a banker. People either kowtowed to me because they wanted to borrow money, or they avoided me because they didn't pay it back."

"What is 'kowtowed'?"

"To bow down to someone, as if he is a king."

Charlotte wrinkled her nose. "I don't think people should kowtow."

"But some people do, and always have, and likely always will. At any rate, I was a kind man, decent and hard-working. I tried to help those who came to me. Some I refused to lend money because of their inability to repay the bank. Some I had to foreclose." He paused, a sad expression crossing his face. "I disliked denying or crushing their dreams and needs, but it was my job."

She wrote this down while he stared sorrowfully at the tabletop and turned the room cold with his sighs. If he sighed much more, she'd have to put on a jacket.

"Do you think any of those people wanted to, um,

well, you know…kill you?" she asked as gently as possible.

He jerked up his head. "Apparently so! I'm dead, aren't I?"

"There's no reason to get huffy," she said, feeling rather huffy herself. "I'm trying to help you, remember?"

He fiddled with his bow tie. "Of course. Of course. Pardon me."

She wished he wouldn't be so touchy. "Tell me the names of anyone who might've wanted to hurt you."

He paused, staring into space. "I will have to think about it. It has been a long time, you know."

All these years, he'd done nothing but sit in the kitchen and feel sorry for himself. Surely he remembered the names of people who caused him trouble. But, maybe dead people had a lot on their minds.

"Do you remember what you were doing before…you know, when…" She made a slicing gesture across her throat. He winced and touched his collar protectively.

"I remember that Minerva had not poured my coffee yet, so I was going to do it myself." Charlotte wondered if he ever forgot anything that had to do with food or drink.

"And someone shot you? Or stabbed you? Was your coffee poisoned and you keeled over dead?"

"No! I was hit on the head." He rubbed the back of his skull and winced as if it had just been clunked.

She wrote this down. "What were you hit with?"

He slid a glance toward the marble rolling pin on the counter. She followed his gaze.

"Someone killed you with a rolling pin?"

"I don't know what it was. But I ended up right there." He pointed to a place on the floor near the stove. "Dead as nails."

Charlotte slid sideways in her chair to eye that part of the floor again. She wished it held the clue to what happened to him. She turned back to him.

"Did anyone ever threaten you? Did you get any suspicious letters or phone calls?"

"I don't recall that I did. My seck-a-tree took care of all the mail."

Charlotte paused in her note-taking. "Your what?"

"My seck-a-tree."

"What's that?"

He reared back. "Do businessmen no longer have seck-a-trees to handle correspondence, accounts, errands, and suchlike?"

"You mean *secretary*?"

"That's what I said." He sniffed hard enough to pinch his ghostly nostrils together.

"You have an odd way of speaking," she said. "Where are you from?"

"I was born right here in Park City, but as a young man I spent some time in the theater. I learned to adapt a more cultured speech."

"Hmm." She decided not to tell him his 'cultured speech' sounded phony-baloney. She was beginning to get used to it. "So your *sec-re-tar-y* took care of your mail at work, but what about here at the house?"

"Oh, Minerva always fetched my mail and placed it on the little table in the front hallway."

"Was Minerva your wife?"

"Certainly not. She was my cook and housekeeper."

"And you trusted her?"

"Of course I trusted her. She wouldn't have been in my home otherwise." He seemed outraged by the mere suggestion.

"Mr. Abernathy," she said and paused to choose her words carefully. "If someone murdered you, it might have been someone you trusted."

He blinked at her as if he'd never considered this.

"So did anyone ever send you a threatening letter? Something like 'I'm going to whack you on the head.'"

"No, never." He fiddled with his bow tie, clearly agitated.

She wrote this down, then leaned forward. "Did this Minerva person—"

"Mrs. Minerva Van Elder. And if you're about to suggest she might have killed me, you may go right upstairs to that dusty attic and think about the absurdity of such a notion."

She scribbled down the woman's full name then looked up and frowned at Mr. Abernathy. "I'm suggesting nothing like that. I'm just asking questions." She leaned forward. "That's what investigators do. Ask questions."

He pulled on his shirt cuffs, smoothed his vest, and cleared his throat. "Well, then. Pardon me."

She eyeballed him for another few seconds, then asked, "Do you think Mrs. Minerva Van Elder or your secretary might have kept mail from you? Maybe something that held a threat they didn't want you to see?"

"Gracious, no! Minerva and Miss Emma Stamp—Miss Stamp was my seck-a-tree—were paragons of virtue and propriety. Why, I believe Minerva would sooner bob her hair than take something that did not belong to her—which is also why I know she'd never hurt me."

"Bob her hair? You mean cut it?"

He nodded, his round eyes a little buggy and nervous. He cast a glance at the coffee pot.

"Oh, how I wish I could have a nice cup of coffee or tea." He met Charlotte's eyes. "Just because one becomes a ghost does not mean one has steady nerves ever after. No indeed."

"Then you don't need coffee. My mom drinks coffee all day long, and all that caffeine is one reason she gets so uptight."

"You use peculiar words, especially for a little—er, young lady."

Charlotte refrained from rolling her eyes. "So would these 'paragons of virtue' steal your mail?"

He wagged his mouth open and shut like a dying fish. "Of course not! And I am beginning to resent the inference that these women were dishonest."

"I apologize, but as I said, I'm just trying to find out what happened."

There was a silence, then he said, "Very well. Continue."

"Good. So…moving on. Let's talk about phone calls."

"What about them?"

"I assume you had a telephone here at home and at the bank?"

"We were quite modern. Of course, we did not have anything like that new-fangled box there." He pointed at the old black wall phone. She supposed if you lived a hundred years ago, anything fifty years old might seem 'new-fangled.'"

"Did anyone ever call up and threaten you over the telephone?"

He shook his head. "If they had, Jane Fillmore would have overheard. She listened in to everyone's conversations."

Charlotte wrote down the new name. "Who's that?"

"Why, the telephone operator, of course." He said it as if Charlotte should have already known about Ms. Fillmore and her job.

Charlotte had seen telephone operators on old movies. They wore big headphones and had wires and stuff everywhere, and all of it was plugged into a big panel of lighted holes on the wall. She could not imagine living in a world that needed telephone operators.

"Did you get along with your neighbors?" she asked.

"The business took most of my time, so I rarely socialized, but there was…." He paused and his expression turned faraway as he looked into the past. "Well, there was that one young woman who moved in across the street. Catherine Anders."

His voice turned soft, and his eyes got misty and dreamy. Charlotte recognized that look from the same sappy, silly movies that had telephone operators. She knew what it meant.

"And you fell in love with her," Charlotte said.

He blinked, as if he couldn't believe she'd said such a thing.

"Why would you say that?"

"Maybe I'm psychic." When he frowned, she said, "Just kidding. It was that look on your face, all mushy and sweet."

"I wasn't aware I ever looked mushy and sweet."

"Uh huh. Did that girl across the street know how you felt about her?"

He was quiet for a while. "Perhaps not." He looked away. "She had a suitor. I think *he* knew I fancied Catherine."

"Aha! What was his name?"

"I have shoved his name from my memory," he sniffed. "And what do you mean 'aha!'?"

She made a note about Catherine Anders and her boyfriend. "Jealousy, of course. Maybe he saw you flirting with Catherine –"

"I never!" He pulled himself straight and tugged on

his cuffs. He brushed the sleeves of his jacket as if flirting was disgusting dust that clung to him nearly a hundred years later. "I was always a perfect gentleman!"

"I'm sure. Anyway, jealousy is a theory, and I'm keeping it on my list. Try to unshove his name from your memory, please."

He wrinkled his nose as if the memory stank. "Perhaps it will come to me."

Charlotte chewed on her pencil and reread her notes. She heard Mom coming downstairs. A moment later she entered the kitchen and went straight to the coffee maker. Charlotte hoped Mom hadn't overheard her talking to Mr. Abernathy.

"I really should move this coffee maker upstairs, but there's only the one outlet and the power strip is already full. I hope I haven't overloaded it…." Mom was a worrier, no doubt about it. She sipped and looked at Charlotte over the rim of her cup. "Have you had your breakfast, honey?"

"Yes, ma'am. Have you?"

"I'm just taking a break."

Taking a break meant using the bathroom and filling her coffee mug. At lunch, she'd nibble on a banana and sip more coffee at her drawing table or sewing machine or computer. She got so busy sometimes, she wore her pajamas all day and ate cereal for dinner.

"You should eat something," Charlotte said. Sometimes she felt *she* was the mother.

Mom poured more coffee in the half-empty cup and grabbed the newspaper from its place in front of Mr. Abernathy.

"I'm fine. I need to glance over the 'people pages' and find out who's important in this town."

"Why?"

"Because those are the people who will pay me to design clothes for them." She grinned and wriggled her eyebrows at Charlotte as though this was some kind of grand plan. "See ya later," she said as she turned and went back upstairs.

Charlotte eyed the empty doorway, trying to remember the last time she and Mom had a regular, normal meal together. Quick trips through the fast-food places as they moved and settled in did not count.

She turned to Mr. Abernathy who stared forlornly at the place his newspaper had been.

"Did anyone ever break in here and steal anything? I mean, while you were alive?"

"Noooo," he said slowly, thoughtfully. "Well, wait a minute. My silver letter opener went missing. It was engraved with my initials, C.A.A. Given to me by my professor of dramatic arts at the university."

"Someone stole *a letter opener*?"

"It disappeared, so I assume it was stolen. I kept it on my desk in the study here at home."

"This house doesn't have a study. Maybe you lost the letter opener at your office in the bank."

"This house most certainly *does* have a study!" he

43

said, drawing himself up and tugging on his vest. "In the southeast corner, just off the parlor. It faces the street."

"There is a living room facing the street. No parlor, no study."

"I beg to differ!" He scowled and twitched, and he huffed enormous cold breezes across the table.

"Mr. Abernathy, I believe you," she said quietly, trying to soothe him. "I'm sure it was built that way, but the man who owns this house now told us it was turned into apartments years and years ago. Some walls have been knocked down and other walls built, and over the years, owners rearranged the spaces a bunch of times. Probably the only thing that's still the way you remember it is my weensy closet upstairs and these awful old kitchen cabinets."

Far from calming him, her words stirred his agitation even more. "Oh dear. Oh dear oh dear oh dear."

Charlotte started to get him a glass of water, then remembered ghosts don't drink. She thought his face couldn't look any paler, but it did. In fact, he began to fade. Was he going to vanish completely?

When he looked normal again, she heaved a sigh of relief. "Golly, Mr. A. You nearly went away again."

"Yes. Yes, yes." He nervously patted himself down as though checking to see if all his body parts remained. "Fading away has only ever happened when I go outside this room. This is the first time it's happened in the kitchen."

"Maybe you shouldn't get upset then. Maybe that's

why you fade. You should stay calm and stay put."

"Yes. Yes, indeed."

She watched him closely, just in case it started to happen again, although if it did, she would be helpless to stop it.

"I always suspected Alfred Crum," he said unexpectedly.

She blinked and reached for her pencil. "You think he killed you?"

"Alfred? Mercy, no. But he likely took my letter opener. He had a collection of them from all over the world." He leaned toward her a bit as if about to spill a secret. "Apparently they weren't enough for him. He envied *mine*. Tried to get me to give it to him, as a gift!"

"That was pretty nervy of him."

He sat back. "Indeed." He sighed and spread his hands in a gesture of helplessness. "But, of course, I have no proof it ended up in his collection, especially as he moved away in 1925 and died in an explosion soon thereafter."

Charlotte winced. "That's gruesome."

"Yes."

"And there's no way he killed you to get your letter opener—which would have been a terrible reason to do so."

Another sigh from Mr. Abernathy, and Charlotte shoved the thought of explosions out of her thoughts.

"Think hard, Mr. A. Was there anyone who profited from your death?"

The way he twitched in his chair and fiddled with his tie, lapels, and glasses, there must have been someone he knew. At least he didn't start to fade away this time.

"There is one name that comes to mind," he said.

Charlotte tightened her fingers around the pencil and held it above the paper, ready to write.

CHAPTER FIVE

“Horatio Ewing Lawson the Second,” Mr. Abernathy said.

“*Horatio*?”

He grimaced. “Yes. I shall never forget that name.”

“I can see why. Tell me about him.”

“Well, my dear girl, he was a charmer. Are you too young to understand that?” He squinted his right eye and lifted his left eyebrow. He looked just like someone in a comic book.

“Of course not. Go on, please.”

“He could charm a stone into thinking it was a pool of water. That’s how he became successful. I relied, of course, on my hard work and honesty to get ahead.” He preened a bit, smoothing his lapels and looking smug.

“So did he charm you into something?” she asked.

“Certainly not!” he snapped, drawing himself up straighter than a broomstick. “Well, not after I got to know him. It's often hard to know if someone is deceiving you until you get to know them."

"I agree," she murmured. Olivia often tended to butter up someone she didn't like just to get what she wanted. Was that being charming? If so, charm was something Charlotte preferred to avoid.

Mr. Abernathy continued. "Not only did he work at the bank with me, but we also invested in a property together, a fine hotel downtown—the Clairmonte. But, he did *not* charm me. I saw the investment as a grand opportunity, so I approached him. He had the capital, after all."

"Was there any reason Mr. Lawson the Second might want to harm you?"

He waved one hand dismissively. "My half of the hotel ownership would go to him, should I die, but he knew without my overseeing the management, the Clairmonte likely would have closed. As it was, the hotel thrived under my supervision."

As Charlotte wrote this down, she wondered if she should tell Mr. Abernathy the Clairmonte was now a rundown old relic. She decided to say nothing about it, because it would upset him. He'd probably start to fade again.

"Now, Mr. Abernathy." She looked him squarely in the eyes. "I want you to think hard. Is there anything else I should know? Anything at all? Anyone you neglected to mention or forgot about?"

His round eyes grew narrow and thoughtful. He

rubbed his chin as he stared at nothing.

"Many years have passed, you know," he said.

"No kidding. But will you think about it? A name or a place or a reason someone might want to bump you off…anything at all."

He winced at her words but nodded. "Surely."

She read over her notes, then closed the notebook and stood up.

"Where are you going?" he asked, looking dismayed.

"Hey, if you want me to solve this mystery, I can't do it hanging around in the kitchen with you. I'm going upstairs to see if Mom will let me use her computer."

He looked puzzled, and she realized there had been no such thing as computers in 1929.

"Computers are machines that have everything you need. Well, everything that's ever been put in books, plus—"

"Oh, now, really!" He reared back as if she'd poked him in the chest with something sharp. "There's no such thing!"

"But it's true. Surely other people who've lived here used their phones or laptops where you could see them." She paused. "Didn't you notice?"

A scowl creased his face, and he waved one hand dismissively as if her question made no sense. "You cannot tell me there is a machine containing information to help you solve the mystery of my death."

She blew out a deep breath and tried not to be

annoyed. "I hope I can find something on a computer, yes."

He looked completely unconvinced.

"Just trust me, Mr. Abernathy," she said. "I mean, you have nothing to lose, right?"

He sighed. "Well, you do have a point."

His eyebrows, lips, and cheeks drooped as if his face was melting, as if he didn't want her to leave. After all, she was the first person ever to talk to him since he died. She wanted to pat his shoulder to show she understood but figured her hand would go right through him.

"Hey, we're friends," she said with a reassuring smile. "We'll have a lot to talk about, every day."

A bit of hope shone in his eyes. "You mean that sincerely?"

"Yes, and I'll tell you everything that I discover about your case. But now, I'm going upstairs to use the computer. I'll be back."

She hurried upstairs and stopped in the open door of the sewing studio. Mom was muttering under her breath, counting. Charlotte waited until she'd scribbled something on a piece of paper.

"Mom? Okay if I use the computer?"

"What?" She glanced over her shoulder. "Oh, no, not now, honey. I need it today. But why don't you go to the library? It's nearby, and I'm sure it has computers for people to use."

Charlotte recalled seeing the two-story gray and white building with all the windows just a few blocks away.

"May I go there now?"

"Sure. Take my phone," Mom said. "But no calls, not even a text, except in an emergency."

"But—"

She gave Charlotte a don't-argue-with-me look. "We have to watch our pennies."

Charlotte grimaced. "A text would only cost a penny or two. Maybe less."

"No."

Charlotte tucked the phone into the pocket of her jeans. She couldn't even call or text Olivia or Chloe because Mom would probably check to see if she had.

"Okay. Emergencies only," she muttered.

"Good." Mom kissed the top of her head, then turned her attention back to her work.

Charlotte picked up the newspaper from the desk. Mom wouldn't miss it. At least not right away. In her bedroom she brushed her hair and slid her feet into sneakers.

Downstairs, she laid the newspaper in front of Mr. Abernathy. "Now you can finish it."

A smile spread across his face, the first one she had seen.

"Mom won't let me use her computer," she added, "so I'm going to the library."

"The library!" He smiled and his face lit up. "Yes, a good place to find information." He reached one hand toward her, and a cool breeze shivered between them. "Bless you, my dear. Bless you."

It felt *good* to be doing something for someone else. She beamed back at him, feeling happier than she'd been in a long time. So what if her only friend in Park City was a ghost in peculiar clothes who used big words no one understood? At least she had one friend. And so did he.

She picked her pencil and notebook and put them in her empty backpack, thinking of another way she might be a friend to him. Just the idea made her smile.

"See ya later, Mr. A!"

Charlotte paused on the sidewalk to adjust the strap on her backpack. She glanced at the house across the street. It was old and shabby, just like all the other houses in her neighborhood.

The small, one-story house with peeling white paint squatted between to two Victorian houses like a toadstool between two half-wilted lilies. Thick weeds choked out the grass, and one of the front windows had been replaced with a square of cardboard. At least that house wasn't school bus yellow like the one where she lived.

She tipped her head to the side and studied the place, wondering what Catherine Anders' house had looked like when she had lived there. More than likely, the woman's home had been as big as the others on this street. What had happened to it? Had it burned down or something?

Mr. Abernathy had looked a lovesick hound dog as he talked about Catherine. She must have been elegant and beautiful. Had she been kind and sweet, or aloof and snooty? Funny and fun? She wondered why Mr. Abernath—

"Hey, kid!" The voice fractured her thoughts. She blinked to clear the made-up images of long ago from her mind. Sometimes, when she was daydreaming, she could get almost as lost as Mom.

A boy in droopy olive green shorts, baggy black t-shirt, faded red cap, and sloppy sneakers stood on the sidewalk on the other side of the street. He held a skateboard in one arm. He was the same boy who'd called out to her earlier when she'd picked up the newspaper.

"What're you lookin' at?" He wasn't smiling, and he didn't sound very friendly.

"That little house right there."

He glanced behind her at the yellow monstrosity she now called home. "You live in that old thing?"

She nodded. He sneered.

"Then you got no reason to be lookin' down your nose at anything. Put your eyes back in your head and stop gawkin' at our house."

Her mouth flew open. "I can look at any house I want to!"

"Yeah? Well, stop looking down your nose at ours."

"I wasn't looking down my nose at anything!"

"You were too. Like you think you're better than

everyone else."

"I did not! I was just—"

He stepped off the sidewalk and into the street. "I saw the cops at your house. You're probably one of those trouble-making mean girls at school."

"That's how much you *don't* know. I just moved here!"

He set the skateboard in motion, hollering over his shoulder as he rode away. "You and your friends stay on your side of the street, kid."

"I don't have any friends around here, anyway!" she yelled after him.

She stuck out her chin and strode away. Not only did she live in the ugliest house on a street full of ugly houses, the first kid she'd met close to her age was a complete nitwit.

CHAPTER
SIX

Inside the Park City Public Library, several computers sat on two long tables near the check-out desk. Every computer had someone sitting in front of it, tapping a keyboard. A bunch of people clustered behind them, waiting their turn. Charlotte stared at them in considerable dismay.

She figured she'd be standing there all day, waiting for her turn at a computer.

She approached the check-out desk where a young Asian man with shining black hair and bright smile checked out books to a woman. His blue name tag read "Shoji Tsuruoka."

When he finished his task, he turned his smile to Charlotte. "How may I help you?"

"I need to do some research, but...." She motioned toward the busy computer station.

He glanced at the users tapping on keyboards.

"You'll have a wait a while, but maybe if I knew what you were looking for, I could find a book that would help."

"Yes, please. Something about the old days here in town. Is there a history book about Park City in the early 1900s?"

"You're in luck," he said with a big grin. "We have old newspapers on microfilm dating all the way back to 1890."

"Microfilm? What's that?" She imagined tiny little cameras but couldn't figure out how they would help.

"Film strips with pictures of every page of the newspapers. Lucky for you, we kept them, even after we joined the digital age." He laughed and beckoned to her. "Come with me."

"Thank you, sir." As he came around the desk, she asked, "How do you pronounce your name?"

His smile grew. "So-gee. Sah-roo-kah. Call me Shoji."

She stuck out her right hand. "I'm Charlotte. Nice to meet you."

They shook hands, then he led her to an alcove where two viewing machines sat on a table. They looked like old computer monitors.

"The microfilm is in boxes in this cabinet next to the readers," he said as he slid open a drawer and took out a small box. "Each box has a roll of this film on a spool." He took out a roll and showed her the slippery dark film about as wide as her two thumbs together.

Once Shoji showed her how to thread the film through the machine, turn the handle on the side to move the film, and use the viewer, he asked, "Got it?"

She nodded. "I understand."

"Great! I'll be at the front desk if you need anything."

"Thank you."

Soon she was whirring through the film so quickly her vision blurred, but she kept turning the little handle until she found Mr. Abernathy's death on page three of May 1929's last newspaper.

"C.A. (Clarence Albert) Abernathy, prominent banker, was found dead in his home this morning by his cleaning woman, Minerva Van Elder. Miss Van Elder reported that she walked into the kitchen to find her employer on the floor, dead from a head wound. Police say Abernathy likely hit his head in a fall and died from the injury. A full obituary will be published in next week's paper."

She read it one more time, slowly. Mr. Abernathy was stuck in his kitchen because he fell and hit his head?

"That's it?" she said out loud. "How can that be all?"

Hadn't he been murdered? Wasn't there any kind of investigation into foul play? She sat back in the chair, folded her arms, glaring at the machine. She huffed and glowered, then finally rolled the film forward to the following week's issue.

The obituary was on the front page, complete with a photo of an unsmiling Mr. Abernathy. He looked exactly as he had sitting at Charlotte's kitchen table. She read the three short paragraphs—Mr. Abernathy had been fifty-one when he died, never married, no brothers or sisters. He had been "esteemed in the community" and "after a short graveside service he was interred at the Rock Church Cemetery."

So. That was that. He had died from an accident in his home, and they buried him. Boom. Over and done with. No mention of how important he'd been to the town, or anything. Not one word about foul play, a suspect, or anything. Poor Mr. Abernathy hadn't even had a proper funeral.

"Give me a break!" She didn't care that she was supposed to be quiet in the library. This was just too much.

"Having trouble?" Shoji entered the alcove, his expression concerned.

"No trouble with the machine," she said, "but don't you think it's sad someone only had an itty-bitty memorial service and an itty-bitty write-up in the paper? It's almost like he never existed."

Shoji frowned slightly and his mouth turned down. "That's really sad. Didn't he have any family or friends?"

"I guess not." Charlotte sighed and turned back to the screen. "But he *was* an important person in Park City back then."

Shoji looked at the grainy image on the microfilm screen. "Is that the man you're reading about?"

Charlotte nodded. "Mr. Abernathy. He built the house where I live now."

Interest crossed his face. "I see."

"He died there," she told him in a low voice. "In the kitchen."

"Did he?" He leaned closer to the screen and read the name. "C.A. Abernathy, eh? That name's familiar." He thought about it a few seconds, then snapped his fingers. "I know where I've seen it before. It's on a plaque in the bank. He was one of the founders."

"That's what he said." Too late Charlotte realized what had just come out of her mouth. "I mean, the newspaper said it. That he worked at the bank, I mean."

Shoji read the obituary again then straightened. "He passed away a few months before the crash of '29," he said. "That was in October. Black Friday and everything that happened afterward was hard on the money-handlers. It was the start of the Great Depression."

Charlotte refused to tell this nice librarian that, instead of moving on to the afterlife, Mr. Abernathy was stuck right here in Park City, in his own house. He'd probably think she was a kook.

She pulled the notebook out of her backpack and handed over the list of names she'd written down earlier. If she found out more about the people on that list, maybe she'd learn more about Mr. Abernathy.

"Have you ever heard anything about any of those people?"

He read the names aloud. "Minerva Van Elder,

Emma Stamp, Jane Fillmore, Catherine Anders, Horatio Ewing Lawson the Second." He shook his head. "I haven't. But Mrs. Shreve, the town historian, would be the one to ask. She has an office right here in the library." He gave Charlotte a hopeful smile. "You want to talk to her?"

She grabbed her backpack. "That would be awesome."

She trailed him into a small office on the other side of the library. It smelled of peppermint, coffee, and Vicks VapoRub. Behind the desk, a thin woman with tall white hair studied her computer monitor without noticing they were in the room. The round glasses perched on the tip of her sharp nose reminded Charlotte of the ones Mr. Abernathy wore.

"Mrs. Shreve?" Shoji said softly.

She barely turned her head to look at them. There was no warmth in her eyes or a trace of a smile on her face.

"Yes?"

Shoji handed over the notebook. "This young lady is researching local history. She was hoping you might be able to tell her something about the people on this list." He turned to Charlotte. "Mrs. Shreve has an eidetic memory. That means she can read something a time or two and remember it all."

"That's great!" Charlotte gave the woman a big smile. "I wish I could do that."

Mrs. Shreve gave her a chilly look then silently

scanned the list of names. She removed her glasses and ran her gaze over Charlotte, from the top of her head to the sneakers on her feet. She wore no expression. According to Charlotte's dad who was a detective, if you couldn't read a person's face, they were usually hiding something or up to no good.

"There used to be some Van Elders over on Spruce," she said at last, "but I believe they moved. Emma Stamp was ninety-four when she died. That was in 1986." A glance up, then back to the list. "Never heard of Jane Fillmore. Anything else?" She returned the list to Charlotte.

Anyone else might bow or drop a curtsy, but Charlotte was not the bowing, curtsy-dropping kind of girl. Instead she met Mrs. Shreve's eyes straight on.

"What about Catherine Anders? And Horatio Ewing Lawson the Second?"

She wanted to ask the sour-faced woman what was the good of an eidetic memory if you overlooked things, but she didn't want to get kicked out of the library for being rude or something. As it was, Mrs. Shreve tightened her already tight lips and curled both her hands. She sniffed as if something smelled stinky.

"Horatio passed away on October 27, 1929, two days after Black Friday. I suppose his heart couldn't take the stock market crash. Catherine died in 1958." She stared at Shoji and Charlotte as if they were responsible for the stock market crash *and* both deaths. "Now, if you'll please excuse me, I have work to do."

Charlotte looked squarely into Mrs. Shreve's pale brown eyes and refused to back down.

"Ma'am? What do you know about Clarence Albert Abernathy?"

The woman gave one long blink. "His name was not on your list."

"No, ma'am."

There was a tiny little pause before she replied, "C.A. Abernathy also died in 1929."

Charlotte tried hard not show her annoyance. "But do you know *anything* about him? Anything at all?" She glanced at the stuffed shelves of books in that small office and pointed at them. "Surely there's something in one of those...."

The woman straightened her spine even more. "I know nothing more than I've told you. Now, I really must get busy." She put her glasses on and turned to her computer.

"Do you know how he died?" Charlotte persisted.

The woman pressed a couple of keys then peered at Charlotte over the top of her glasses. "I believe he was found dead in his kitchen where he had fallen. Most likely a heart attack."

"But maybe it wasn't a heart attack," Charlotte said.

Mrs. Shreve crimped her lips into a thinner line.

"Did Park City have a lot of murderers running around loose in 1929?" Charlotte asked.

Mrs. Shreve scowled and pinned her frosty gaze on Shoji. "With what have you been filling this child's head?"

"She's interested in some of the townspeople of the past, ma'am. Since you're the town historian, I thought you were the best person for her to meet."

The woman studied Charlotte as if looking for a terrible flaw. She sighed as if she was exhausted by hard work. Answering questions couldn't be considered hard work, not if you're the town historian and supposedly an expert.

"I see. Well, it's best to leave the dead buried."

What a creepy thing to say. Mrs. Shreve seemed uninterested in the lives of people who had lived in Park City all those years ago. Apparently, they were just facts and dates to her. In Charlotte's opinion, someone else ought to take over the job of town historian.

"Now," the woman said, making a shooing gesture with both hands. "Leave me to do my work, or I'll have to have a word with your supervisor, Mr. Tsuruoka."

"Yes, ma'am," he said, so polite he practically glowed with courtesy. "Sorry to have bothered you."

Shoji led Charlotte out of the small office. Be-fore he closed the door, she saw Mrs. Shreve watching them, her eyes narrow, her face pinched and pale.

"She knows something, but she's not telling," Charlotte whispered as he shut the door.

Shoji smiled. "Could be."

"I'll just have to find out what I want to know in some other way."

CHAPTER
SEVEN

Before Charlotte left the library, she asked Shoji, "Do you have some recent news-papers that you're going to get rid of?"

"We recycle them. Someone comes to collects them every couple of weeks." He gave her a curious look. "You know, Charlotte, there won't be any information in those papers about the people you're researching."

Telling him she was getting the newspapers to help a ghost was a dumb idea. "I know, but may I have some of them anyway?"

"Sure. I'll see what I can find."

By the time Charlotte turned down Timberline Avenue on her way home, the strap of her bulging backpack cut painfully into her shoulder. She hoped Mr. Abernathy wanted to read newspapers from Park City, Little Rock, and Memphis because Shoji had given her as many as she could stuff into her backpack.

A steady, soft rumbling from behind caught her attention. She glanced over her shoulder. The rude boy who lived across the street rode his skateboard toward her on the sidewalk.

"Hey, kid. You still eyeballin' houses that don't belong to you?"

She said nothing but walked faster.

"Hey!" he said, catching up to her.

She slid a sideways look at him. Up close he didn't appear so bad. He was clean, and he had nice hazel eyes.

"You really are stuck up, aren't you?" he said.

She lifted her chin. "I'm not stuck up, but you sure are hateful, yelling at me when you don't even know me."

He winced, as if she'd thrown something at him. "I don't usually yell at people."

"Could've fooled me, all that hollering you did." She stopped and moved her heavy backpack from one shoulder to the other.

"Say, that looks heavy," he said. "Want me to carry it for you?"

"Why would I want you to do that?"

"Because I'm a boy. I'm strong. Look." He flexed his arm muscles.

"Yeah, so? I'm a girl, and *I'm* strong." She resumed walking.

He jumped around in front of her and walked backwards, never taking his gaze off her. "Hey, listen, I'm sorry I was, y'know, rude and loud and stuff earlier.

I thought you were going to make fun of my house and everything, and well…." He shrugged. He really did look sorry.

She slowed. "Why would I make fun of your house when my own house is so awful?"

"I know, right? I mean, we're both kinda stuck living in these ugly old houses."

They stopped to look at both houses, noting size and color and ugliness.

"At least your house isn't as yellow as egg yolks," she said.

"Yeah. But yours isn't so small you nearly bust the seams."

"I bet yours doesn't have kitchen cabinets that won't stay closed."

"I bet yours has a toilet that doesn't leak," he said.

"Yours doesn't have a dark staircase so narrow and steep it's practically like going up a ladder in the middle of the night, even in broad daylight."

He looked impressed. "Really? Cool!"

She wrinkled her nose. If he ever saw that staircase, he might not think it was cool. But then, he was a boy, and boys seemed to like creepy places.

"If you weren't going to say something mean about my house, why were you looking at it, anyways?" he asked.

She shrugged the shoulder without the backpack. "I like to think about things, so I was thinking about people who lived here in the olden days, in these houses. And I was thinking that yours is way smaller that all the rest of them, and I wondered why."

"The house that used to be there, y'know, in the olden days? Granny said it burned down a long time ago."

"When was that?"

"I dunno. Before she was born." He flipped his skateboard belly-up to spin the wheels. They made a hissing sound.

"Have you lived there a long time?"

"Since second grade," he replied, "and it was old and ugly then."

He spun the wheels again and watched them turn.

"Do you know anything about the house that burned down?" she asked.

He looked up and frowned a little. "No. Why would I?"

"Aren't you interested in it? Don't you want to know about who used to live there?"

"No. Who cares, anyways? They're dead or gone somewheres else now." He looked down at the skateboard. "You skate?"

She shook her head. "I've never tried."

"You wanna learn? I can teach you." He looked and sounded eager.

She shifted the backpack from one shoulder to the other. "Maybe someday. I have stuff to do."

He sneered. "Are you chicken?"

Charlotte hated anyone to think she was weak or scared.

"No, but I'm on a mission."

He gawked at her. "A *mission*? You mean like those door-to-door church people?"

Was this boy dumb, or what?

"I mean like I have something important to do, and I don't want to get sidetracked by riding around on that thing." She pointed at his skateboard.

"It's not a thing. It's my board." The way he spoke, as if the skateboard were his best friend, Charlotte knew she'd touched a nerve.

"Sorry," she muttered.

He spun the wheels again. "You got a name, kid?"

"Yes. Do you?"

They battled with their eyes, trying to stare each other down. She relented first.

"I'm Charlotte."

"You can call me E.Z."

She blinked in surprise. "Easy?"

"E period, Z period. E.Z. My real name is Ezra Zachariah, but don't you *ever* call me that."

"Okay." Charlotte understood completely. Her first name was Coco, after the designer Coco Chanel. Unlike E.Z., though, she wasn't going to mention it. If she never told him, he could never call her that.

The strap bit into her shoulder, reminding her that Mr. Abernathy would love to have the newspapers. "I have to go now."

"On your mission?"

"Yeah."

He looked down at the ground and rolled a loose pebble with his shoe. "Okay, then. See ya around, kid."

"Charlotte. Please don't call me 'kid'."

He glanced up, nodding. "Yeah, whatever. See ya."

He took off on his skateboard, and she went to the house. At first, he'd been surly and snotty, but then he'd been kinda shy and sweet. The hateful boys at her school stayed hateful. Then there were the boys so desperately sweet that they got her nerves. Only a few were right in the middle between being nice and being obnoxious.

One thing was sure: she'd never met anyone quite like E.Z. Had she just made another friend?

CHAPTER
EIGHT

Hot and sweaty from walking home with such a heavy load, Charlotte went into kitchen where it was cool. She dragged the heavy backpack off her shoulder and plunked it down on the table.

Mr. Abernathy looked at her, his face awash with eagerness. "Did you find out who killed me?" he asked.

"Not yet."

His face sagged. "No?"

"I've only started looking. But you'll like this." She opened the backpack and began to unload the newspapers in front of him. "These are from last week."

The gloom lifted from his features. He all but clapped his hands. "Excellent!"

Looking at his smiling face, something occurred to her. "Mr. A, do you think you could read a book the way you do newspapers?"

"No one has ever left a book here for me to look at.

Five, six, seven...." He was counting the number of papers she'd laid out.

She opened the cabinet where Mom kept a few cookbooks and took out the one titled *101 Favorite Cookies*. She put it on the table.

"Try," she said.

Mr. Abernathy stared at the red and white book as if trying to move it with his mind. He reached one plump hand with index finger extended, touched the book and moved it. He looked at Charlotte with a huge smile on his face. If anyone had walked in right then, they would have seen the book slide across the table by itself.

"Yay! Mr. A, this means I can bring you books to read."

"Yes! And look at all these papers. Oh, I am happy!"

"That's great. I hope you enjoy them." Charlotte turned on the tap and splashed some cool water over her sweaty face.

Hauling that heavy batch of newspapers from the library had made a long, hot, and thirsty walk. She filled a glass with cold, sweet tea from the refrigerator, added some ice then took a long drink. She sat down across from him while he looked with delight at those one hundred and one recipes.

"Thank you, dear child. Your efforts are greatly appreciated."

"I'm glad to help you." She watched him gleefully regard the papers, then said, "By the way, the notice of your death was in the local paper right after you died."

He lifted his gaze. "Of course it was. Do you have

one of those papers in this stack?"

"No, they were on microfilm."

His mouth flew open, and she knew he was about to ask her about microfilm. She waved one hand to stop him. "I'll explain that to you another time. But anyway, your picture and obituary were in the next week's paper."

He leaned forward. "Did you read it?" he asked eagerly. "Was it written well?"

"I read it."

"And?"

She hesitated. "It was a bit short."

"Short?" He sat up straight. "*Short?*"

Charlotte wished she hadn't told him that. "It was very well written."

He said nothing for a few moments, then, "There's some comfort in good prose, at least. Was my funeral well-attended?"

"Um. I...er, the paper didn't mention how many people were there."

"I see. Well, I'm sure the entire town turned out." He smoothed his hair as if a town full of people were eyeballing him at that moment.

Charlotte opened her notebook and hoped he asked nothing else about his funeral.

"I talked with Mrs. Shreve," she said. "She's the town historian."

He fiddled with his bow tie. "And what did she tell you?"

"Not much. She's not very friendly."

"Hmphf! Disagreeable woman," he muttered as if he had been there with Charlotte and Shoji while they tried to get information from her.

"She certainly was. And her office smelled weird." She wrinkled her nose. "Anyway, I mentioned those names you gave me, and she—"

A knock at the front door interrupted her. "Excuse me, Mr. A."

E.Z. stood on the front porch. He held a bottle of Pepsi Cola in each hand.

"Hi," she said through the rusty screen. She hoped he wasn't there to talk her into skateboard lessons. She wasn't in the mood for that.

"Hey. You want a pop?" He showed her both bottles.

Charlotte liked sweet tea better than cola, but she nodded.

"Sure." She opened the door. "You want to come in?"

"Thanks." He stepped inside and handed her a cold, damp bottle.

The drink hissed as she unscrewed the cap. She took a sip, and the icy sweetness slid all the way down her gullet to her stomach.

"That's good," she said, stifling a burp.

He nodded and took a slug from his own bottle. "Yep. I put 'em in the freezer a while back so they'd get good and cold. You leave 'em in too long, though, they bust all over everything."

E.Z. looked around the empty, dismal front room, his gaze sliding from the cracked ceiling to the peeling paint to the grungy worn-out green carpet.

"Don't you have chairs or anything?"

They did back home in Macomb. It was nice furniture, too. Soft and comfy and pretty. But she didn't want to mention any of that to him. He'd just want to know details, and she wasn't in the mood for that, either.

"Mom says we don't really need furniture in this room. She's trying to get her business started, so she's mostly in her studio upstairs. I hang out in the kitchen or my room."

"What kind of business?"

"Clothing design."

"Oh yeah? My Ma works at Honey-B's. It's kinda like a bar and kinda like a restaurant." He paused. "Does your mom spend much time with you?"

She thought of Mom, busy with her patterns and fabric from sun-up to sundown, and how she didn't like to be interrupted.

"Not much," she said.

"Yeah, mine neither. I guess moms have better things to do than spend time with kids." He didn't sound sad. Just matter-of-fact, as if he was used to it the same way she was used to it. They stood in the empty living room, sipping their drinks. She heard his stomach growl.

"You want some fruit or a cookie or a sandwich or something?"

His eyes brightened. "Sure! A sandwich would be awesome."

In the kitchen, Mr. Abernathy watched the pair, his round eyes growing large as he stared at E.Z. The air grew chilly.

"Hey," E.Z. said, "you got an air conditioner in the kitchen! That's awesome. We only have a small one in the front room."

She wasn't about to mention that cold air was created by the ghost at the table.

"What would you like, peanut butter or salami?"

"I like 'em both, together."

"Really? Ew."

"It's good. You oughta try it sometime."

She took salami from the refrigerator and got the bread and peanut butter from the cabinet. She shut the door but of course it swung open again and stayed that way, like a broken shutter.

"Stupid door," she muttered.

E.Z. closed it and watched it fall open. He did it again, and it swung open once more.

"Huh. I could fix that for you. Probably."

She smiled at him. "That would be awesome. These cabinet doors make me crazy."

"I betcha this house is haunted. Some dumb ghost probably wants the door open. It probably wants to stare at the peanut butter."

Charlotte dropped the knife she'd just taken from the drawer. Mr. Abernathy cleared his throat loudly and glowered at E.Z.

"Tell that impertinent young man to pull up his

trousers before we see the entirety of his drawers." He sniffed, high and mighty.

She frowned at him and shook her head slightly.

"A house this old probably has a bunch of ghosts hiding in the closets," E.Z. said, "or down in the cellar, scaring each other."

"You have a ghost in your house?" she asked uneasily.

He shrugged. "I don't know. Granny probably wouldn't let one stay. She's mean."

Charlotte hesitated a moment, then asked, "So you believe in ghosts?"

He shrugged again. "I dunno. Maybe. But I guess you gotta be dumb to believe in them, huh? I've always thought that if ghosts are real, they must be stupid. I mean, why else would they hang around after they're dead?"

"Upon my word!" Mr. Abernathy snapped.

He got up from the table, marched to the open cabinet and slammed the cabinet door so loudly that she and E.Z. jumped like a pair of startled chickens. He stood next to the cabinet with his arms folded across his chest, glaring at E.Z.

"I didn't know you could do that!" Charlotte yelped before she could stop herself.

"I didn't do anything!" E.Z. said, gawping at the door as it sagged open again.

She hoped Mom hadn't heard the noise, but her hopes died quickly.

"CHARLOTTE!"

Mom came thundering down the steps, a pencil behind each ear. Her seamstress tape measure hung from her neck like a dead yellow snake.

"What on earth?" she hollered. "That sounded like a gunshot! Are you all right?" She spotted E.Z. and rushed to pull Charlotte close to her. "Who are you?"

Charlotte squirmed, trying to wriggle free of that iron grasp.

"I'm fine," she said. "Mom, please, *stop*."

Mom clung to her. "Did you shoot a gun in this house?" she yelled at E.Z. "Did you—"

Mr. Abernathy slammed the cabinet door again, sudden and loud. Mom gave a little scream.

"I will not have this uproar in my kitchen," he shouted, as if he thought everyone could hear him and would obey.

"I'm sorry," Charlotte told him. "I'll try to…Mom, please let go of me. This is my new friend, E.Z."

E.Z. and Mom ignored each other for a minute to gape at the cabinet door.

"How…wha…." Mom seemed unable to say more. She touched the little gold circlet at her neck as if it might steady her nerves.

"Dude, I'm tellin' you, this place has a ghost!" E.Z. fixed a big-eyed stare on her and her mom. "I didn't touch that door, let alone slam it. I swear it."

Mom looked as if she expected him to produce a submachine gun from beneath his ball cap.

"Mom. Please." Charlotte finally freed herself from that smothering grip. "E.Z. lives across the street. And he did not slam the cabinet door." She shook her arms to get the feeling back in them.

"I'll slam it again to prove your point, shall I?" Mr. Abernathy said, reaching for the door again.

"NO!" she shrieked. His slamming the door again would prove she and E.Z. had told the truth, but Mom would freak out, big time. She said quietly, "I mean, no, he didn't slam the cabinet door. We have a draft in here. It blows from those old windows by the dining table."

"This kitchen always seems cooler than anywhere else in the house," Mom said. "You're probably right, Charlotte."

Mom ran her hands over her hair and felt the pencils. She pulled them out and frowned at them as if she'd never seen such things, then she shifted her attention to E.Z. The smile she offered seemed both apologetic and forced, as if she hadn't made up her mind about him yet.

"I'm Mrs. Franklin."

E.Z. held out his hand and they shook like two grown-ups meeting in church.

"E.Z. Bishop."

"So you're a neighbor?" she asked.

"Yes, ma'am. I live in the little white house across the street." He dipped his head in the direction of his home.

"You're the boy with the skateboard, aren't you?"

"Yes, ma'am."

"What little white house?" Mr. Abernathy said, indignant and frowning. In fact, he had not stopped frowning since E.Z. and Charlotte entered the kitchen.

"Right across the street," Charlotte told him.

"Yes," Mom said. "I heard him, honey." She gave E.Z. a more genuine smile. "I've seen you on that skateboard. You should be careful. And wear a helmet."

"There is no little white house on this street!" Mr. Abernathy insisted. Charlotte did not respond to him this time.

"We're having a bite of lunch, Mom," she said. "You want me to fix you a sandwich?"

"Not right now, thanks. I have a lot to do." Her gaze landed on the pile of newspapers. "Charlotte, where did you get those and why did you bring them here?" Frowning, she gathered them in her arms like a load of laundry.

"No, no, *no!*" Mr. Abernathy wrung his hands and all but hopped on one foot. He stretched out both arms but failed to touch Mom. A blast of cold air shot through the kitchen.

"I picked them up at the library. I'll take care of them." Charlotte reached for the papers, but Mom turned sideways to block her.

"I'm going upstairs. I'll take them with me. They'll be excellent to use for pattern making if I run out of pattern paper. Thank you for thinking of me." She started to walk out of the room, but turned and said, "Nice to meet you, Easy. And I apologize for assuming you were here to cause trouble. It's just that I was so startled."

He smiled at her. Charlotte thought she'd never seen a smile as nice as E.Z.'s. It reached his eyes and made them sparkle. She could look at his smile for a long time.

"That's okay, Mrs. Franklin," he said. "I understand."

He did? No one had ever understood Mom. She figured Mom didn't even understand herself.

"How old are you, Easy?"

"It's E.Z., ma'am. And I'll be fourteen in a few weeks."

She stood there a bit longer, as if she'd forgotten what she wanted to say, but finally went upstairs, taking the mound of newspapers with her.

"She seems nice," E.Z. said.

Charlotte nodded. She hoped her new friend didn't add that Mom also seemed weird.

That's what Olivia and Chloe always said—"I like your mom, but she's really weird." Charlotte knew they were right, but it always upset her when they said it.

"Would you like a glass for your Pepsi?" she asked E.Z.

"Nah. I don't need a glass." To underscore his point, he lifted the bottle and chugged a long drink.

"Well, help yourself to the peanut butter and salami."

"So tell me something," he said after they made their sandwiches and settled at the table.

She figured he was going to ask where her dad was,

or if her mom was nutty, or something like that. She sipped her cola and eyed him guardedly. "What do you want to know?"

"Have you seen any ghosts in this house?"

Her eyes went straight to Mr. Abernathy. He did that thing where he squinted one eye and lifted the other eyebrow as he waited for her to answer.

It would be nice to tell someone about Mr. Abernathy, maybe get some help in finding out who killed him. She could tell E.Z., but she'd only just met him. For all she knew, he might be the town's biggest blabbermouth. Or he might call her nutsy. Or he might get up and go home and never speak to her again.

She moved her gaze from Mr. Abernathy to E.Z.

"Nope."

CHAPTER
NINE

On Friday, Charlotte's father came to get her for the weekend. When he pulled up, Charlotte was glad so glad to see him that tears burned her eyes.

"Do you have everything, honey?" Mom asked from the doorway of her studio. "Did you remember to pack your pajamas?"

"Yes'm. See you Sunday night."

She shot down the narrow stairs, grabbed up the backpack, and ran out the front screen door. It banged like a shot behind her.

"Hey, sweetheart." Dad got out of the car as she flew across the yard to him. He hugged her hard, then took her backpack and put it on the backseat. "You have everything you need? Did you remember your pjs?"

Now, see? Right there. Almost exactly word for word what Mom had said a minute ago. That just proved her dad and mom should be together, not separated by over a hundred miles.

"I have everything." She looked up at him, into his warm brown eyes. He was tall, so she had to look up quite a way. He must have been driving with the car windows open because his dark, curly hair was messy.

"Tomorrow we'll go to the mall and get you some stuff to leave at the house, then you won't have to bring anything with you."

He looked across the lawn toward the house where Mom stood on the top step of the porch, her arms folded across her chest. She chewed her lower lip as if worried.

"Hi, Jen," he said.

"Hi," she replied so quietly that Charlotte wondered if her dad heard.

Instead of getting into the car, he took Charlotte's hand in his and they walked toward the house. Mom shifted from one foot to the other. Why was she so uneasy? Was she afraid to talk to Dad? Was she afraid of being alone in the house after Charlotte left?

"Come to dinner with us," Dad said. Charlotte's heart bounded with hope. It would almost be like a date, sort of.

Mom's eyes widened, and she took a step back. "Why, David."

"'Why, David,' what? You look fine, Jennifer. As pretty as ever. And we're just going to the Pizza Place."

"I don't think that's a good idea." She fingered the little gold circlet necklace.

He looked at the necklace then said, "Why not? You love pizza."

She glanced at Charlotte. "I…I just don't think it's a good idea for us to … to … ."

"To have dinner?" he asked.

"No. Be together." She snapped out these last two words with a kind of fierceness that made Charlotte lose hope. "Y'all just go on now and have dinner and have a nice drive and a nice weekend, and I'll see you Sunday, Charlotte."

She gave Charlotte a quick kiss on the cheek, then hurried into the house as if she'd been standing outside in her undies or something.

He stared at the closed door in silence.

"You want me to go see if I can talk her into coming?" she asked. It was nice that her dad was a romantic person. Maybe he'd be able to win back his wife. But Charlotte's mom seemed to have nothing but fashion design in her head, or her life, and Charlotte doubted there was room for anything else.

He shook his head. "If she doesn't want to come, she won't. Your mother is a stubborn woman."

He smiled to take any sting out of his words, but Charlotte knew he was hurt.

They walked to the car and when she was inside with her seatbelt fastened, she glanced across the street. E.Z. was standing on the sidewalk in front of his house, rolling from side to side on his skateboard, watching them. Charlotte pressed the button to open the window on her side.

"I'm going with my dad. I'll see you Sunday," she

called to him as they drove past.

He lifted one hand, then took off down the sidewalk on his skateboard, not looking back, not even once.

"You have a boyfriend already?" Dad always teased her about every boy she ever looked at, even if she accidentally glanced at one. She sighed.

"He's just a neighbor. Good grief."

He stopped the car, right in the middle of the street. "You want to introduce us? You want to tell him goodbye?"

Charlotte loved her dad a lot. She was happier than she could say to be able to spend the entire weekend with him, but right then, she wished a hole in the earth would open up so she could jump in.

"No! Please, Dad. Just drive."

"You sure?"

He was grinning like a monkey, but she knew he'd give E.Z. the daddy-cop's once-over stare if he got close enough.

"Positive." She scrunched down in her seat and hoped neither E.Z. nor anyone else saw her and her dad sitting in the middle of the street like two goofs. "*Please. Let's go.* Good grief."

"Whatever you say." He drove on, snickering as if the whole situation was a big fat joke. Charlotte stayed hunkered down out of sight until they turned off Timberline and headed to the Pizza Place.

She lost her embarrassment as they talked and ate cheeseburger pizza, her favorite. Her dad wanted to add stuff to it, like sausage, mushrooms, onions, green peppers, and black olives and who knows what all, but the thought of a pizza with all those toppings together made Charlotte shudder.

Later, when they neared Macomb and the evening sky was dusky dark, she said, "So, Dad? Olivia is having a sleep-over tomorrow night for her birthday."

"Is that so?"

"Yep. May I go?"

"To a party your mother grounded you from?"

She groaned silently. "Yes."

"No, you may not."

"But I haven't seen Olivia and Chloe in forever."

He glanced at her without a trace of a smile. "I'm sorry, honey, but your mother grounded you from going."

"How'd you know that?"

"She emailed me."

She folded her arms and glowered. "You two can't agree on anything else, but you agree on this."

"We agree on a lot of things," he told her. "And one of them is raising you. Being grounded is your punishment for making a nonsense call to 9-1-1. That's a serious thing, kiddo."

She turned toward him. "It wasn't nonsense!"

"You want to tell me why you pulled such a prank?"

She huffed. "It was not a prank, I promise you."

Maybe her dad would be more understanding of Mr. Abernathy than Mom had been. He'd kept his cool about Janelle Dunmark, and he'd never blamed Charlotte for Janelle's ghostly pranks. Charlotte needed to talk about Mr. A with someone.

"If I tell you why I called 9-1-1, will you let me go to Olivia's?" she asked hopefully.

"You are going to tell me why you made the call, no doubt about that." He wore what Charlotte called his "cop face." It was hard, expressionless, watchful, and waiting—waiting for the guilty person to confess. "And you are *not* going to the sleepover," he added so firmly she could practically see the words as he spoke them.

She stared straight ahead and said nothing for a while. She finally glanced at him.

He smiled and ruffled her hair as if she were a little girl. "Anyway, you're here to spend the weekend with your old man, remember?"

She nodded. "I know. And I'm glad to be with you, Daddy."

After they'd been home for a little while and she'd put her things away, Dad handed over a cell phone. "Go ahead and text your friends. Or call them."

She grinned so big her cheeks ached. It had been so long since she'd seen or talked to Chloe or Olivia, she decided to call and hear their voices.

"Hi, Olivia!" she squealed the moment her friend

answered.

"Hey."

"It's me. Charlotte."

"I know."

"Happy birthday!"

There was a short silence, then Olivia muttered, "Thanks."

Charlotte frowned. Olivia had changed over the last year, but she had always liked talking on the phone.

"Is something wrong? Are you sick?"

"No."

Another silence. This time a long one.

"Um … I'm sorry, but I can't come to your party."

"Yeah, I know." Olivia went from sounding bored to sounding ticked off. "Your *mom* texted me. That was really lame."

"I know, but she won't let me use the phone except for emergencies."

"What about the laptop? You could have used it."

"She won't let me. It's for business only, or schoolwork."

The silence stretched so long Charlotte wondered if her friend had hung up until she heard Chloe's voice saying something.

"May I speak to Chloe, please?"

"You know what, Charlotte? You moved away, and Jodie McMillan took your place in our group. So…tough luck being you, I guess."

"Wait! What did you say? Who…?" Dead air met

her ears. The whole conversation, such as it was, mystified her completely.

Olivia had sounded angry. She hadn't wanted to talk, didn't even make an attempt to be nice, but maybe cutting off Charlotte had been an accident. Charlotte called her back immediately, but Olivia didn't pick up.

She sent a text to both girls.

"We're busy," Chloe texted back.

"Make friends in Park City," Olivia wrote.

"What's wrong?" she tapped and sent, but neither girl answered. A sharp stab, like from the tip of a knife, gouged her inside. She thought her friends would have been glad to hear from her after all this time. Instead, they acted like she'd done something wrong. They didn't even try to understand. She clenched her jaw and refused to let even a single tear form in her eyes.

"Dad!" She found him in the kitchen making grilled ham and cheese sandwiches. "Dad, my friends hate me."

"Now why would you say that?"

She swallowed hard so her voice wouldn't break and told him what had just happened. "If mom hadn't grounded me and if she'd let me text Olivia instead of doing it herself like she thought I was a baby, then they wouldn't hate me."

Her dad wiped his hands on a paper towel and met her eyes. "They don't hate you. Maybe they're a little mad right now. Let them be mad. They'll get over it."

"But it wasn't my fault."

"They'll get over it, sweetheart. And if they don't,

then you'll know they really aren't very good friends. In the meantime, try to make new friends in Park City. Moping around won't help. No one wants to hang out with a droopy killjoy." He turned to the stove and poked at a sandwich with a spatula. "These sandwiches are just about finished. Pour us some iced tea, okay?"

The last thing Charlotte wanted was to be a killjoy, so she kept fighting back her tears and confusion. She gave him a smile. Maybe she should've expected Chloe and Olivia to act the way they did. Still ... that little stabbing ache inside her was going to be there for a while.

When she and Mom lived with him, Dad would get called in to work so often she'd only see him occasion-ally. This weekend, though, they hung out together *all* weekend. It was great to spend that much time with each other.

He'd said nothing else about that 9-1-1 call, but he probably would, sooner or later. That's how he was. He'd let things ride until he felt it was the exact right time, then he'd bring it up. She wasn't worried about talking to him, though. He *listened*.

Saturday evening they sat in patio lounge chairs on the back deck of the house while burgers sizzled on the grill and filled the air with smoky barbeque. He had taken her to the mall that morning and bought her some new summer outfits. She held her legs straight out so she could watch the light twinkle off her new sparkly flipflops.

"How come you aren't working this weekend?" she asked.

"I talked to my captain. She'll call me only if she absolutely has to. She has seven kids of her own, so she understands." He smiled at her. "Are you having a good time, just the two of us?"

"I like hanging out with you, Dad. We don't have to do anything special to have a good time."

He got up and flipped the burgers. They sizzled and sent up a noisy whoof of fragrance. Charlotte's stomach growled.

"I want the days that you stay here to be good for you," he said. "I'm sorry you're grounded from the party, but I'm glad you're spending this time with me."

She shrugged. "Chloe probably would've wanted to paint her toenails the whole time, and Olivia would probably want to do nothing but text boys anyway."

After their dinner of burgers, chips, coleslaw, and chocolate chip cookies, they stretched out side by side in the loungers. Dad had turned off the lights so they could look up at the stars and watch the lightning bugs flit from place to place.

It was such a quiet, companionable time that Charlotte said, "Dad, if I ask you something, will you think I'm nutty?"

He turned his head, and she could see his eyes shine softly in the dark. "I could never think you're nutty."

"Even if what I say is all weird?"

"Say it."

She gulped in a big breath, then asked, "Do you believe in ghosts?"

"You could say I have an open mind." He smiled. "Why? Is there a ghost in that old house your mother moved you to?"

"Yes."

"I see." He was silent for a few seconds, then he asked, "Are you afraid?"

"No. His name is Mr. Abernathy and he's been stuck in our kitchen since 1929."

She paused to gauge his reaction.

"Go on," he said.

"I'd been hearing the windchimes again, like I always do." When he simply gave an encouraging nod for her to continue, she told him as much about Mr. Abernathy as she knew. "I feel sorry for him," she concluded.

When Dad said nothing, she grew uneasy. "Don't you believe me?" she asked.

He sat up on the edge of his lounge chair, turned to her, and said, "Yes, I do."

It felt like someone had just lifted a heavy weight off her chest. "You don't think I'm just making him up?"

"No, sweetheart. I believe you."

"Mom thinks I'm making him up. He was sitting right there in front of her, and she couldn't see him. I tried to tell her, but she said for me not to have another

Janelle Dunmark episode, then she grounded me from Olivia's party because I called the cops."

"But if you'd been hearing the windchimes, you knew he was likely a ghost. Why did you call the police?"

"Because he *could've* been an intruder, not a ghost."

"Then you did the right thing to call 9-1-1."

"I know, right? Mom wouldn't have been nearly as upset if he'd been just a plain ol' robber or something."

"Aw, now."

"No, really. She hollered at me, and said I was just trying to cause a ruckus. That police officer chewed me out like you wouldn't believe. It was way embarrassing."

"Didn't you explain to your mom? Did you tell her you'd been hearing wind chimes?"

She shook her head. "You know how she is, Dad. Remember how she got when Janelle Dunmark showed up. And when the others began showing up...well, when I mentioned them she'd get really upset. If I'd have even mentioned the chimes, she would've freaked out." She paused, swallowed back a lump, and blinked hard one time. "She doesn't want to listen to me. At all. About anything, *ever*."

"I know it seems that way sometimes, but—"

"No, Dad. It *is* that way."

He reached out and squeezed her hand. "Cut your mom some slack, honey. She's doing her best. And she's trying to find herself."

Find herself? She'd heard Mom say those two words a million times in the last year, but Charlotte still didn't understand what she meant.

"While she's looking, couldn't I come back here and live with you after I solve Mr. Abernathy's murder?"

Dad tightened his grip on her hand, not painfully, but reassuringly. "It'd be great to have you here. I hope you know that." He paused and tipped his head to one side until she gave a half-nod, half-smile, and half-shrug. "But you also know I'm not home much of the time. Plus, your mom really needs you right now."

She puffed out air between her lips. "She's so wrapped up in her designs and patterns that she barely knows I'm there."

"Aw, now. She knows. Like I said, cut her some slack. Let her get her feet on the ground with this new venture."

She wrinkled her nose. "I don't have much choice."

"Sorry, kiddo. I wish things were different right now, but I think your mom and I can work things out one of these days."

Hope, like a butterfly, fluttered in her chest. "Really? When?"

"At some point. When the time is right. But we have to be patient." He let go of her hand, settled back in his lounger, crossed his legs at the ankles, and locked his hands behind his head. "Now, let's look at the stars, and I'll tell you something you didn't know."

CHAPTER
TEN

"**Y**ou never met your great-grandmother, Ellen Claxton." Dad's voice filled the night between them and made Charlotte feel safe and loved. "She died long before you were born."

"Was she your grandma, or Mom's?"

"Mine. She had a...gift."

Little prickles stood up on the back of Charlotte's neck. She heard the faraway sound of wind chimes, so faint she thought she might have imagined them.

"A gift? Like mine?"

He nodded once. "Like yours."

"Mom doesn't believe in my gift."

"Sweetheart, it isn't that she disbelieves; she's that way because she's frightened."

"Of my 'gift', you mean?"

"Yes. You know what a worrier she is," he said. "I've known your mom since she was sixteen years old.

She has always been a nervous, jittery person. Don't resent her for that. Her perception of spirits is that they are here to hurt you, and until she finally believes that's not the case, she'll stay scared. She'll pretend your ability to see those spirits isn't real."

"But that's silly!" she said. "They've never hurt me or even threatened to. They're just annoying, popping up here and there, watching me like I'm one of the animals in the zoo. Most of them never even say a word. The only one to cause problems was Janelle Dunmark, and she went away a long time ago."

"You've told your mom this, right?"

"Yes. But she doesn't listen."

"I'm sorry she doesn't," he said.

They sat in silence for a bit, then Charlotte sighed a sigh so deep that Mr. Abernathy would've envied it. "I wish she'd get over being jittery," she said. "One thing's for sure. I don't consider this…whatever it is, a *gift*. I think of it as a nuisance. An awful nuisance that makes no sense, and I wish I didn't have it."

He turned toward her again. "Maybe you should learn to appreciate this nuisance of a gift—use to it help others. I think that's why you have it."

"To help others? Even dead others?"

He nodded. "Your great-grandmother did."

"She did?"

Charlotte had tried to ignore the gift for so long, she wasn't sure she *could* appreciate or use it.

A sudden chill breeze blew across them, and the

chimes were louder. They sounded nearby. An expression flicked across her dad's face, and he shot a quick look around them. Charlotte sat straight up, every cell in her body prickling like crazy. She knew what was happening.

"Do you have the gift, Daddy? Do you hear the wind chimes?"

He shook his head. "No, honey. But I feel the cold air."

Charlotte looked around, saw nothing in the dark except the normal things, silvered with moonlight. No spirits were lurking, hanging around in the yard, staring at her. There were a few times when she'd heard wind chimes and felt the air stir, but no one appeared. Maybe no one would show up tonight.

She sat back and looked at her dad. "Tell me about Ellen Claxton, please."

He shifted a little in his chaise. "She lived quite a way from us, so we only saw her during the winter holidays. I remember her as kind, always smiling. She liked to give hugs. My mother told me that Grandmum had 'visions' all her life."

"Visions?"

"She'd see people who'd passed away, or sometimes, she'd visualize an event before it happened."

Charlotte let this soak in. "Were you afraid of her?"

"Not at all. She was funny and sweet. She loved to cook, and she made the best cakes and pies you ever tasted."

"But she saw dead people?"

"That's what my mother said. Well, she said Grandmum saw spirits of—"

"Dad," Charlotte interrupted. "Do the neighbors ever come over here at night?" She pointed at the tall, dark-haired woman walking toward them from the house next door. Even in just the moonlight, Charlotte saw she was young and beautiful. The lady was smiling in a very special way at her dad.

"No, they don't."

Charlotte pointed. The woman gave her a little wave and smiled brightly. "Right there."

The wind chimes fell silent, and the summer night air turned cold. Charlotte didn't need to glance at Dad to know he was frowning, peering into the shadows, looking for someone he would never see.

"Who are you?" she asked the woman.

"I'm your great-grandmum." She stopped near the bottom step of the deck.

Charlotte raked her gaze over the woman. "Whoa. You're Ellen? But you're so young and beautiful."

Ellen's smile held so much sweetness as she ascended the steps and she exuded such a good feeling, Charlotte wanted to go to her, hug her. But of course she didn't. She *couldn't*.

"This is how I felt when I died—young and beautiful. In fact, young and beautiful is how I felt every one of my eighty-two years, even though my mirror told me I was old." Her smile grew. "I never believed that mirror, anyway."

Charlotte couldn't help but grin as she stared at her great-grandmother. She glanced at Dad, who had settled back in his chaise, watching her with curiosity. She pointed.

"Ellen is here. Gosh, Dad, she's a looker, tall and slim, with long, curly dark hair."

He laughed. "And a million-dollar smile?"

"You can see her?" she asked eagerly.

"No. But I've seen photos of her."

"I'm only here for a moment, Charlotte," Ellen said. "Your mother needs you, even more than you and your father realize."

Charlotte lost her smile. "No, she doesn't. She doesn't need either of us."

Ellen stretched out a hand as though to touch her. "Sweetheart, try to understand. She's a frightened soul desperately looking for her place in life."

"She has a place. She's my mom! She's Dad's wife. *She has a place.*"

"Of course she does. She loves your father—"

"I know! How could she not?"

"His work has kept them apart so much that she's had time to think of what else she'd like to do. And she loves being your mother. She always will, but one day before long, you'll be grown and out on your own, and she's preparing herself for that."

Charlotte grimaced. "But does she have to be so ridiculous?"

"She's not being ridiculous. She's lost. She doesn't know how much she needs you."

"Yes, she does. To fix her meals and bring her coffee and keep the house tidy."

Ellen's eyes filled with compassion. She tipped her head to one side. "She needs someone to embrace her. To listen to her. To tell her she's on the right path, if she stays true to it. All those stray thoughts shooting around in your mother's head make her seem distant and unloving. They are what prevent her from fulfilling her dream. You need to talk to her, every day—"

"But she doesn't want to talk to me. And she doesn't listen."

Ellen continued as if Charlotte hadn't interrupted. "Talk to her, every day, when she comes downstairs for coffee in the afternoons. That's when she's ready to listen."

"But—"

"She loves you, Charlotte. Far more than you realize."

"But what am I supposed to say to her?"

Ellen began to fade. "Your heart knows what to say, sweetheart. Listen to it."

"I'll do my best but wait! Just another minute." She stretched out one hand, trying to catch the woman before she completely disappeared.

The ghost paused, almost gone, shimmering like moonlight on water.

"What about Mr. Abernathy? Do you know him? Do

you know who killed him? What am I supposed to do about him?"

"Trust your father to help you with that one. He's extremely clever, your papa. And whatever you do, don't neglect your mother. Or your new young friend. He needs you too."

"So many people need me," Charlotte said, feeling overcome and scared.

"Yes, but you're a strong young woman, and you're up for it." Ellen turned her shimmering, nearly invisible smile to Charlotte's dad. "My goodness, didn't David Anthony Franklin grow into a handsome man? So much like his grandfather."

And with that, she was gone.

Charlotte sat, frozen in time and space, until Dad gently cleared his throat. Slowly, as if her body was made of thick honey, she turned to look at him.

"That was Ellen," she whispered.

"I thought so."

"She's gone now."

He nodded.

"She walked up so natural, I thought she might be a neighbor."

He smiled. "Want to tell me what she said?"

Charlotte swallowed hard, and flexed all her muscles, trying to make everything feel normal again. "Daddy, it's like she's been watching and listening to us."

"I imagine she has been. Watching over you,

helping you get through the days when things are tough."

"Like a guardian angel?"

"Something like that, yes."

"Wow." Charlotte thought about this for a while. "She wants me to spend more time with Mom. Do you think I can make Mom hang out with me? Even if I ask her to, she's going to say, 'Don't bother me, now, Charlotte' like she always does when I try to talk to her."

He patted her hand. "I know. But see if you can think of a way to keep her with you for a while. For instance, ask her about what she's working on. Be interested in it."

"But, ew, Dad. There's nothing as boring as a conversation about basting and top-stitch and French seams."

"To you, maybe, but not to your mom. It might not be as boring as you think, if you really listened to her. Ask questions. Maybe you'll learn something. Besides, I know you love your mom, and you want her to be happy."

It seemed that Great-Grandmum Ellen still lingered, just out of sight, encouraging Charlotte to listen to her dad. Of course she loved Mom. Of course she thought sewing was boring. But maybe he was right. And maybe if she could figure out something they had in common....

Like she'd done with Mr. Abernathy.

Something warm stirred inside her, and she knew her thoughts were on the right track, finally. For the first time since she and her mother had moved from Macomb, Charlotte felt better.

"I'll do my best," she promised.

The next day, as Dad drove her back to Park City, they talked more about finding out what happened to Mr. Abernathy.

"I would be so much easier if I could get online," Charlotte said. "Couldn't you get Mom to let me have my laptop and my phone? I know she has prepaid a certain amount so usage is limited, but I wouldn't use very much."

Dad shook his head. "Sorry. But unless and until your mother relents, she is determined to make her own way."

"But if I was careful about it and only used a few minutes, she'd never know—"

"You'd know. And I'd know. Besides, years ago no one had laptops or cellphones, and they got along just fine without them. You're going to have to survive with paper and pen for a while."

She pulled a face. "That's what I've been doing."

She took a lot of notes as she rode back to Park City. By the time he dropped her off at the yellow house— without going inside and talking to Mom—Charlotte had a list of questions her dad suggested she should ask if she found anyone who could tell her anything about Mr. Abernathy.

Mom gave her a hug. "Did you have a good time?"

She nodded. "Yes, ma'am, I did."

She remembered what Ellen and her dad had said. She gently plucked a loose bit of coral-colored thread from Mom's hair.

"What did you do while I was gone?" she asked.

"You want to see?"

"Sure."

Mom gave her a happy smile and grabbed her hand. "Come on. I'll show you."

Upstairs, instead of going into the sewing studio, she led the way into Charlotte's bedroom. On the bed was a pair of khaki cargo shorts and a sleeveless coral top with a gathered waist and buttons down the front.

"Oh, wow! Those are cute!"

Charlotte dropped her backpack on the floor and picked up the blouse. The fabric was slippery and cool feeing between her fingers.

"Try everything on. I think it'll fit." Mom touched the gold circlet at her neck and looked a little anxious, as if Charlotte might not like the outfit.

"When did you make this for me?"

She nodded. "Night before last, I woke up around midnight with this idea in my head, and I could not dismiss it. So I got up and made it for you."

The shorts and top fit Charlotte's lanky frame perfectly. She threw her arms around Mom and hugged her hard.

"Thank you for thinking of me." She blinked hard and pulled back. "I love them."

Mom beamed, happier than Charlotte had seen her

in a long time. "I'm glad. Are you hungry?"

She shook her head. "Dad and I stopped at the Taco Place in Fielding."

"You look tired." Mom stroked Charlotte's hair and tucked a strand behind her ear. "Why don't you get a bath and pile into bed?"

"I will. Just as soon as I get a little apple juice."

Mom smiled and patted Charlotte's cheek. "Okay, honey. I'll be in my studio, if you need me. Come kiss me goodnight before you get in bed."

Gosh. Mom was being a mom. Had Great-Grandmum Ellen talked to her too? Probably not. But maybe her mom had always been a more of a mom than Charlotte realized.

Knowing Mr. Abernathy waited for her in the kitchen, she hurried down. He smiled happily when she entered.

"I'm so glad you're back," he said. "I've missed our conversations."

"I will tell you about everything tomorrow," she promised as she filled a small glass of apple juice.

He looked disappointed, but said, "Of course. A growing child needs her rest."

"The good news is my dad gave me some tips for helping find out who killed you."

The ghost nearly clapped his hands in delight.

CHAPTER ELEVEN

Monday morning, Charlotte woke up later than usual. When she went downstairs, Mr. Abernathy greeted her with enthusiasm. She got the coffee maker going for Mom, then poured herself a bowl of cereal.

"What a dull two days have passed in your absence, child," he said. His gaze fell on her colorful cereal. "What sort of cornflakes is that?"

"Not cornflakes. Lucky Charms." She plucked a green clover from the milk and held the dripping confection up for him to see, then popped it in her mouth. "Marshmallow. Yummy."

"I see," he said slowly, with one eyebrow up as if he didn't quite approve.

She ate quickly without saying much and slurped down the last drops of milk. Mr. Abernathy lost his smile, and a frown creased between his eyebrows. "In light of the fact you are doing me a favor by seeking my killer," he said, snooty-like, "I shall overlook your atrocious table manners."

"I was drinking the milk from my bowl. I didn't lap it up like a dog."

"Is the coffee ready, Charlotte?" Mom called from upstairs.

"Has she been down this morning while I was still asleep?" she asked Mr. Abernathy. He shook his head. "I'll bring it up to you, Mom," she called.

Quickly, she poured cereal in a bowl and added milk to it. She grabbed a spoon and laid everything on a tray. She filled a large mug of coffee for her mother.

"She doesn't always eat regular when she gets wrapped up in her work," she told Mr. Abernathy as she left the room, "so I make sure to take her food. Be right back."

Balancing the tray, she took the steep stairs two at a time and dashed into the studio without spilling or dropping anything. Mom was bent over the worktable, drawing with a thin blue pencil.

"Here, Mom," she said. "Lucky Charms."

"Thanks, honey. Would you bring me coffee?"

"I have it right here. Hey, Mom?"

"Umm?" She never looked up.

"I'm going to the library today, okay?"

Mom said nothing for a minute, then stopped what she was doing and turned to her. "What did you say, honey?"

Charlotte waited until Mom's eyes lost their dreamy

114

expression. "I'm going to the library, if it's okay with you."

Mom nodded. "Sure, honey. That's fine."

"I won't be too long," Charlotte promised.

"That's fine." Mom turned her attention back to her work as if she'd already forgotten Charlotte was there. But Charlotte remembered what Great-Grand-mum and Dad had said and tried hard not to be annoyed as she went to her room.

She put on the new outfit Mom had made, slid her feet into a pair of sandals, brushed her hair, scooped up her backpack and went downstairs. Outside, she fetched the newspaper from its place near the porch and carried it to Mr. Abernathy.

"Here you go. I'll try to arrange it so Mom won't come back downstairs for a while."

She grabbed the coffee pot and carried it upstairs. "Mom, here's the coffee pot for you since I won't be here to bring you more. I made a full pot this morning, so there's plenty."

She glanced up and smiled. "Okay, sweetie. Later, gator. Take the phone. Emergency only."

"Yes, ma'am."

Downstairs, Charlotte poked her head into the kitchen. "See ya later, Mr. A! I promised Mom I wouldn't be gone too long." He was engrossed in the newspaper but looked up and nodded. "What kind of books do you want me to bring you?"

"Nothing foolish. None of those trashy dime novels."

"Dime novels? What's that?"

His mouth flew open, then he snapped it shut. "My dear child, if you don't know, I am not going to tell you."

In her opinion, that was the dumbest answer anyone ever gave to any question ever asked. He turned to his newspaper and said nothing else. She slung one strap of the nearly empty backpack over her shoulder and left the house.

"Hey, kid!" E.Z. hollered from his front yard.

"Hey, Easy," she called back, glad to see him.

"Dude, don't call me 'Easy'."

"Dude, if you're gonna call me 'kid'...."

"Okay, okay." He grinned as he loped across the grass toward her with his skateboard under one arm. "Where you going?"

"To the library."

"How come?"

"To get a couple of books for someone. You want to come along?"

"Sure." He fell into step beside her. "I'll carry your backpack, if you'd like."

She smiled. "It's not heavy but thank you. Say, do you have a computer or cellphone I could use? If you do, I could—"

He shook his head before she finished.

"Sorry. I wish I did, but Ma can't afford it. Even if we did have a cell or even a laptop, Granny would lay hold of it and never let me use it."

She pulled a face. "Yeah. I guess we're in the same boat."

"You mean you don't have anything, either?"

"Nope. Well, Mom's cell, but I can only use it for emergencies, like if I get run over by a car. And my laptop and phone are back in Macomb."

He huffed. "Charlotte, we must be the only two kids in this town who are living in 1975."

"You got that right."

"Well, at least we're in 1975 together," he said with a grin.

She laughed.

A minute later, he asked, "Did you have a good time with your dad?"

"Yeah. He's cool."

"So you like him?"

"Of course, I like him. I love him. He's awesome."

He nodded, jumped on his skateboard and skated a few yards, then hopped off. "Must be nice."

"What? Liking my dad?"

"Having a dad to like."

"You don't have one? Not even a stepfather?"

"Stepfathers." He grunted the word, scowling. "Ma's boyfriends. But I don't have a real dad. Well, I have one, y'know, but I don't know who he is or anything."

"I'm sorry to hear that."

He shrugged, and the frown lifted from his face. "It's all right. It's just the way it is." He skated ahead a few more feet, spun the board to face her, then hopped off and walked beside her again, tucking his skateboard

117

under one arm. "Tell me about your old man."

"He's not an old man," Charlotte said. "He's my dad."

As they walked, she told him about her father, what he looked like and how he laughed and how he used to make up songs about her when she was little. Talking about him made her happy and sad at the same time.

"He's a detective for the Macomb police force."

E.Z. stumbled a little when she said that. "For real?"

"Yeah. Why?"

He looked uncomfortable. "Cops are scary."

"Not unless you're doing something you shouldn't."

"There was a cop at your house the other day. Was that your dad?"

"No." She thought fast for a way to explain about why the policeman showed up that morning. "He was, um, well, he was checking to see if we were okay."

E.Z. stopped walking and pinned a look on her. "Why?"

She was about to tell him it was none of his business but changed her mind. "I thought I saw someone in the house who shouldn't be there."

"Oh."

They started walking again, and she spoke quickly before he could ask more questions. "But there wasn't anyone, so…it was nothing."

"Oh." He sounded a little disappointed. Charlotte figured she'd never understand boys.

"Dad and I talk about cases he's worked on sometimes," she said, "and he tells me how he solved them. He's really good at his job."

They were nearly at the library by then. E.Z. had a wistful look on his face. "Man, your dad sounds way awesome. I have a feeling my old man is y'know, in the slammer, or maybe he's dead."

Charlotte stopped in her tracks, right in front of the big double glass doors that opened into the library.

"Why do you say that?"

"Ma won't talk about him. Granny gets mad if I ask even a little question, like what color are his eyes."

"I'm sorry. Everyone should know about their own dad."

He shrugged as he pulled open one of the doors, and they went inside. "Yeah. Well." That was all he said as he looked around the place, his eyes wide and curious.

She spotted Shoji Tsuruoka at the checkout desk and waved at him. His grin widened when he saw E.Z. She figured he thought they were boyfriend and girlfriend. Her face grew hot.

"Do you know what a 'dime novel' is?" she asked E.Z.

"Nope. Why?"

"I'm not supposed to get one." She led the way to the checkout desk.

"Hi there, Charlotte! Here to do some more research?" Shoji's smile included E.Z.

"Sort of. What are dime novels?"

"They were books published a long time ago,

printed on cheap paper. Adventure stories, westerns, big game hunting stories, that sort of thing." He glanced back and forth between them. "Where'd you hear about 'dime novels'? That's not exactly a hot topic for kids."

"I want to get some books for a friend, but he said no dime novels."

"Is he an older gentleman?"

She nodded. "Really old." If he only knew how old! "Do you know what his interests are?"

"Banking."

Shoji's black eyebrows went up. "*Banking*?"

"Whoa," E.Z. said, wrinkling his nose and forehead. "Who wants to read about banking?"

"I know, right?" Charlotte thought about Mr. Abernathy and how long he'd been trapped in the kitchen. "Maybe he'd like a book about people and inventions over the last hundred years or so. And a book about computers that will be easy for him to understand."

"Let's see what we have." Shoji walked with them to the American history section and helped Charlotte pick out some books. E.Z. watched them, but he didn't say much. When Charlotte would show him a certain book, he'd just glance at it and nod. Obviously, this outing bored him, but it couldn't be helped.

They found a simple book about computers that Shoji said almost anyone could understand. She hoped that applied to a person who last saw the real world in 1929. Another thing—Mr. Abernathy had been sour far too long. He needed to laugh.

"How about something funny an old guy would enjoy?" she asked Shoji. Her brain clicked with an idea. "Maybe a mystery with plenty of laughs?"

Shoji's face lit up. "I know just the thing." They followed him to a large section labeled *Mysteries*, and he pulled a book off the shelf. "How about something by C.W. R. Butterworth. His sleuth is an old guy who gets himself into all kinds of hilarious situations."

Charlotte wasn't sure Mr. Abernathy would want something hilarious, but the front cover convinced her to take the book.

Shoji tapped the man on the cover. "That's the detective, Mango Riptorn."

"Mango Riptorn?" E.Z. hollered. "That's worse than my name."

"You're not supposed to yell in the library," Charlotte said, trying hard not to giggle as they went to the front desk. She checked out the books, slid them into the backpack and buckled it. E.Z. took it from her and hefted it over his shoulder. She started to protest, but the look on his face told her he really, really wanted to carry it for her. Besides, it *was* pretty heavy, especially as one of the books she chose was a huge coffee table book full of photographs.

As they walked home, he said, "So who is this old dude you're getting books for? Your granddad?"

"No. Just a friend."

"In our neighborhood?"

"Right."

121

"Mr. Jenkins?"

She shook her head.

"Old Man Whittaker? I saw him once, looking out his front window. His face was like, y'know, wrinkled up and yellow." He snickered a little. "Dude, he scared me. I thought he was a ghost or something."

Charlotte thought of Mr. Abernathy. His face was neither wrinkled nor yellow. Except that time he tried to go upstairs and faded out—he'd looked a little odd-colored then.

"I doubt Mr. Whittaker is a ghost. He's probably just old and sick."

"Yeah. Probably."

They'd almost reached home when he said, "I'm thirsty. You wanna soda pop?"

Something cool to drink after their walk sounded good. "Do you have any sweet tea?"

"Nah. We only have pop or beer."

"*You* drink beer?"

"Are you kiddin'? If I so much as touched a can of it, Ma and Granny would nail my hide to the wall. They don't share their Budweiser with anyone. Ma makes her boyfriends bring their own." He slid the backpack off his shoulder and handed it to her. "I'll be right back."

Without warning, Charlotte felt a strong desire to go inside the little white house. "May I go in with you?"

He shook his head. "You don't want to go in there."

"Why not? You came into my house."

"Yeah, but your house is cool. Your mom's nice,

even though she thought I was causing trouble when I wasn't."

"Mom is usually jumpy and irritable when she's into her work." Charlotte glanced at the little house hunkered on its patchy, weedy lawn. "I want to go inside so I can see our house from your front window."

He scoffed. "Why?"

"You know how you just feel like you need to do a certain thing? I feel like I need to go into your house and look out the window." Charlotte got these feelings sometimes, like someone was telling her to go somewhere and do something. She never felt quite right until she followed-through. Her dad would probably call it a "hunch."

E.Z. took off his ballcap and scratched his head, frowning at the sidewalk.

"Geez, I dunno."

"I know it sounds crazy, but please?"

"Our house is dirty and stuff."

"Listen," she said. "I've been in dirty houses before. I have this friend in Macomb. Chloe. Her father has car and motorcycle parts in every room. One time, he even had a whole engine in the middle of the dining room. It was in there from the time we were in fourth grade until Christmas vacation in the sixth grade."

"Yeah, but ..." He looked at his house as if he wished it would disappear. He cut a sideways glance at Charlotte. "You promise you won't tell anyone?"

"Tell anyone what? That I went into your house?"

"That you saw the inside of it, yeah."

"Sure, if that's what you want. But, E.Z., your house couldn't be as bad as ours before we moved in. It was a pit."

"Just don't tell anyone about ours."

"Cross my heart."

He gave her an uncertain smile. "Okay then."

He took the backpack from her and slung it over his shoulder. She followed him through the grimy front door and into a gloomy living room that stank of stale cigarette smoke, grease, and unwashed bodies. E.Z. might be scruffy, but he always looked clean.

An old sofa on the wall near the front door held a pillow and a neatly folded blanket as if someone took naps there. A big screen television took up half a wall on the far side of the room. On the screen, two big sweaty wrestlers flopped around like dying fish. The sound of grunts and the hollering spectators suddenly grew silent.

An old woman was parked in a worn-out recliner in front of the television. She wore a faded, floral house dress, and her frizzy gray hair nearly reached her shoulders. It looked like she hadn't combed it for a few days. Her feet were bare and dirty.

"Well, worthless," she croaked, "where you been?"

"At the library."

She cackled as she shook a cigarette out of a crumpled pack and lit it.

"What would you be doing at the liberry when you can't read any better than that old cat over there?" She pointed to a plaster cat figure on a cluttered shelf. She ran her gaze from the top of Charlotte's head to her sandals. "Got yerself a girl, heh?"

"Granny," he said, looking embarrassed. "We just came in to get a pop."

"What's your name, gal?"

"Charlotte Franklin, ma'am."

The old woman studied her a moment longer.

"The both of you stay outta my smokes and outta my beer." She drew a long drag from her cigarette, then blew it out slowly, still staring hard at Charlotte. "And outta my room." She pointed the remote control at the TV and the thumping sounds of wrestling resumed.

"C'mon," E.Z. said.

She followed him into a tiny kitchen. The counter tops were spotless, the sink was clear, and clean dishes were in the drainer.

"I keep the kitchen clean, so's we don't get so many roaches. You want Co'cola or Pepsi or Mountain Dew?"

"Mountain Dew," she said.

He opened the refrigerator and Charlotte spotted nothing but cans of beer and soda, and a dried hunk of unwrapped cheese. E.Z. closed the door fast. She glanced around the tiny room and hoped the cabinets held food.

He handed her a can of Mountain Dew. It was nice and cold against her fingers and palm.

"So you want to look out the front window at your house?" He popped the top of his Pepsi.

She nodded, and he led her back into the living room

125

where he pulled opened a set of broken, crooked mini-blinds. Her house didn't look quite so awful from this angle, even though the sun shining on it made the yellow glow like a lightbulb. Maybe, back when Mr. Abernathy first built it, it had not been yellow and —

"What're you doin', you dumb cluck?" the old woman hollered. "Close them blinds!"

"She lives across the street, Granny," E.Z. said. "She wants to see what it looks like from over here."

"You live in that house that's the color of mustard?" she asked Charlotte.

"Yes, ma'am."

"What d'ya want to see it for? It's butt ugly, far away or up close. A few feet ain't gonna change that." The woman shifted her gaze to E.Z. "Bring me a beer." She turned her eyes back to Charlotte. "I wouldn't want to live in something that ugly."

Charlotte closed the blinds. "Then it's a good thing you don't live there, ma'am."

The old woman took the opened beer from E.Z.'s hand. She pinned a hard look on Charlotte. "You sassin' me, gal?"

"No, ma'am."

She held Charlotte's gaze a bit longer, then said to E.Z., "You drink any of this?"

"No, Granny." His voice was quiet and gentle. "You ask me that every time, and you know I never touch your beer."

She took a noisy slurp and said, "You'ns go on

outside and stop botherin' me. Don't come back in here 'til your ma gets home."

"Yes'm," E.Z. held the front door open for Charlotte to go out. "I'm sorry," he murmured as soon as he shut the door. "Granny is kinda cranky."

"Is she always like that?"

"Sometimes worse. It's better if I just do what she wants and don't talk too much."

"Golly, E.Z. I'm so sorry."

He shrugged and took a drink from his can. "It's all right. That's life."

Charlotte did not look at this circumstance as "that's life." There was little she could do to change his home situation, but she could be his friend and they could hang out together.

"Listen, Charlotte, you gotta promise me…"

"Promise you what?"

"That you won't tell the kids at school."

"I promised I wouldn't."

"I mean about the rest."

"About your granny?"

"Yeah, and how I have to sleep on the sofa because I don't have a bedroom, and how I have to stay outside all the time because Granny can't stand the sight of me and stuff like that. All of it. Don't tell anyone, all right?"

She focused her gaze on the Mountain Dew in her hand. She wasn't a crying kind of girl, but E.Z.'s words cut into her heart. She blinked hard.

"It's important nobody knows about anything," he said. "I'm tired of fist fights, so I'm trying to keep a low

127

profile."

"You fight?" She could hardly imagine quiet, polite E.Z. as a brawler. But he was big and strong enough to win.

"Yeah, well. I'm not gonna let anyone push me around just because I don't have the things everyone else has. But I don't like fighting. So if you'd just not tell anyone about...." He jerked his head toward his house.

She looked straight into his eyes. "I won't tell. I promise."

His expression remained uncertain.

"Listen," she said, "how about I share something with you that I don't want anyone else to know? If I tell your secret, then you can tell mine. Will that make you feel better?"

"Is it as bad as...." Again, he jerked his head toward his house.

"It's nothing bad, but it's not anyone's business."

He hesitated.

"Come on over to my house," she said, "and I'll tell you all about it."

CHAPTER
TWELVE

M r. Abernathy looked up as she and E.Z. entered the kitchen.

"Well, I see we have a guest," he said.

She nodded, took the backpack from E.Z. and set it against the wall near the table.

"I hope the books I picked out are all right," she said to Mr. Abernathy. He beamed with interest.

"For that old guy?" E.Z. wiped the sweat off his face with the back of his hand. "Yeah, I bet they'll be fine. What'd you say his name was?"

"I didn't say, but I'll tell you in a bit. First, how about a sandwich or something?"

E.Z. grinned. "Cool!"

She set out the food. "Help yourself. I need to let my mom know I'm home. Back in a minute."

She glanced at the table and saw the newspaper was folded neatly next to Mr. Abernathy's right hand, so she knew Mom had not come down from her workroom.

Upstairs, Mom was pinning cut pieces of muslin on her dressmaker's dummy.

"Hey, Mom. I'm back from the library."

Mom looked up and smiled. "Good! It's a nice day for a walk downtown. Look, honey. Look at this and tell me what you think."

She led Charlotte to the drafting table where a colorful sketch was pinned.

"See what I'm doing? I'm using the asymmetrical lines that are so popular right now, but I'm adding this little detail to give it my own touch." She pointed to a place where the fabric curved softly just below the waist. "Do you like it?"

Although Charlotte failed to share Mom's enthusiasm for clothes and fashion, she did like the sketch.

"Awesome. Is that what you're making right now?"

"Yes. I'm using muslin to be sure everything looks the way I want it to before I cut into the dress fabric. See?"

Charlotte eyed the outfit on the dressmaker's mannequin.

"Great." She wasn't certain if what she saw was good, bad, or regular. She'd have to wait until she saw the real dress. "Uh, Mom, can I ask you something?"

"Sure, honey. What's up?" Mom leaned against her worktable and looked at Charlotte with curiosity.

"Would it be all right if E.Z. had supper here a few

nights a week?"

Her mom looked confused. "Easy?"

"E.Z. The boy across street."

"Oh. Well, I suppose so, if his mother doesn't mind. And as long as he isn't rowdy and loud. But a few nights a week?" She frowned slightly. "Honey, I know it's natural for a girl your age to get a crush on a cute boy like E.Z., but you are only twelve—"

"Nearly thirteen."

Charlotte agreed that E.Z. was cute, but she'd never in a million years say so in front of Mom or Dad.

"Still. Just don't get starry-eyed and foolish."

"For one thing, I am not starry-eyed and foolish. And for another, E.Z. and I are only friends. And besides, you don't understand." She lowered her voice. "I don't think he gets much to eat at his house."

"Oh? How do you know?"

Charlotte picked her words carefully because she did not want to break her promise. "I don't think his mom and grandmother do anything for him. He's kinda on his own, taking care of himself. I think he mostly has soft drinks and not a lot of food."

Mom frowned. "How do you know this? Did he tell you?"

"His mother is gone most of the time, and his grandma is sick or something. So can't he please eat here, at least once in a while?"

Mom gazed at her for a long time as though trying to read her mind. Or maybe her thoughts were lost in another garment design. They often were when she grew still and unmoving that way.

"That's too bad about his home life. And boys his age are always hungry. My father used to say your Uncle Stephen had a hollow leg." She laughed. "But I don't want E.Z. to go without. So yes, he may eat over here from time to time."

Charlotte gave her a hug. "Thanks, Mom."

She ran back downstairs, hoping she'd not said more than she should have about E.Z.'s situation. When she went into the kitchen, E.Z. sat at the table, wolfing down his food. Mr. Abernathy watched with considerable astonishment.

"I don't believe I've ever seen a boy his age eat so much, so quickly," he said. "Surely he'll become ill soon."

"I doubt that will happen," Charlotte replied.

E.Z. stopped chewing to stare at her. He swallowed his food and said, "You don't think what will happen?"

She glanced at the counter where she'd set out the sandwich makings. Everything had been put away, and a plump sandwich sat on a paper towel.

"You ready for this one?" she asked.

"That one is for you."

She blinked in surprise. "You made it for me?"

He nodded, smiling with his eyes because his mouth was full.

"Well, well. There lies within this young man a sense of chivalry." Mr. Abernathy grasped his lapels and pursed his lips, nodding. "And today, his trousers, shabby as they are, do not droop. I must say, however, he should remove his cap when he's inside. And why does he wear it that way? The bill is to shade the sun from his eyes, not the neck."

"All will be explained," Charlotte said. From the look on E.Z.'s face, she knew his confusion would keep growing if she kept talking to Mr. Abernathy. "Thank you for making me a sandwich. What did you put on it?"

"It's a PB and J, and a few chips on the top layer."

She put the paper towel on the table in front of her chair, then poured two glasses of milk.

"I still got pop," he said, lifting his can when she put the glass in front of him.

"I know, but you need milk."

He made a face. "I like Pepsi better."

"C'mon. I'm drinking milk too."

"Okay, then."

E.Z. waited until she popped the final corner of the sandwich into her mouth and finished her milk.

"So what's your secret?" he asked.

Mr. Abernathy raised one eyebrow and looked interested. "Secrets, eh?"

"You'll see," she said to the ghost.

"Yeah. I'm waiting." E.Z. grabbed a couple of paper napkins from the holder on the table and wiped his mouth and hands. He looked at her expectantly.

"Remember when you were here last week and talked about ghosts being in this house?" she said.

"I remember."

Mr. Abernathy leaned forward, his gaze shooting back and forth between the two of them.

She took a deep breath. "Well, there's one in here now, and he's sitting right there." She pointed at Mr. Abernathy. Inside herself, Charlotte cringed, waiting for E.Z. to scoff or laugh or tell her she was lying and walk away.

His eyes widened, and he glanced across the table.

"It's true."

E.Z. squinted hard, trying to see something. Mr. Abernathy straightened his bow tie then moved the newspaper an inch or so toward the center of the table.

E.Z. jerked. "Whoa!"

Mr. Abernathy shoved the paper closer to him. E.Z. blinked hard and looked again. "Did you see that?" he asked.

"Yes. And I see him."

He turned his head. "The ghost dude? You see it?"

"Not it. Him. Yes, I see him as well as I see you."

"No foolin'?"

"Not a bit."

"I knew it," he said, after a long squinting session. He reached out one hand and swept it over the table, poking the air. "The air is cool in this kitchen, but it's cold right there."

He had his hand on Mr. Abernathy's neck, right on the bow tie.

"Do you feel that?" she asked the ghost.

"Not exactly," he replied, "but I must say, it's unsettling to have this young man's fingers probing my person."

"Does he feel me?" E.Z. asked eagerly. She shook her head; he looked disappointed and dropped his hand. "What's he look like? Is he all gross and rotten?"

"No! He's not a zombie."

"I should say not!" Mr. Abernathy straightened his neat cuffs. "Indeed not!"

"Well, is he, like, you know, all pale and creepy?"

Mr. Abernathy glowered. He reached across the table and knocked E.Z.'s cap off his head.

E.Z. yelled and leaped from his chair so fast it crashed backward, making an awful clatter when it hit the floor.

"Charlotte!" Mom hollered.

"Don't mention Mr. Abernathy to her," Charlotte warned a moment before her mom came into the kitchen.

"What happened this time? Honestly, Charlotte, you know I need quiet when I'm working!"

"I'm sorry, ma'am," E.Z. said. "It was my fault. I sorta stumbled backward when I got up, I guess, and knocked the chair over. I'm sorry."

He sat the chair upright and gave her an apologetic smile.

"I see. Well, please, you two try to be quieter for me, all right?"

She got a cup from the cabinet and then looked around as if she'd lost something.

"Mom, I took the coffee pot upstairs, remember?"

Her mom's face cleared. "Oh, yes, of course." She turned to E.Z. "You are more than welcome in our home, but you mustn't be so rowdy inside while I'm working. When you're here for dinner, though, you won't have to tiptoe around." She smiled warmly at him.

"Dinner?"

"You're invited for supper," Charlotte said.

"I am?"

Mom laughed. "Don't sound so surprised, hon. It won't be gourmet, but I can throw together a good taco salad or meat loaf or tuna casserole."

E.Z.'s grin seemed to reach both ears. "Geez. Thanks."

"You're welcome." She started to walk away, spotted the newspaper on the table, and grabbed it up. "Charlotte. What is it with you and newspapers lately? Unless you're reading the paper here in the mornings, please bring it up to me, okay?"

Without waiting for a reply, she went upstairs.

"I do say!" Mr. Abernathy scowled.

"Don't worry about it, Mr. A. I brought you books to read."

E.Z seemed frozen in place. "Mr. A?" he said.

"His name is Mr. Abernathy."

"Clarence Albert Abernathy, if you please, dear girl."

She nodded. "Clarence Albert Abernathy. And this is E.Z. Bishop."

"Tell him I'm pleased to make his acquaintance," Mr. Abernathy said.

"He says he's pleased to meet you."

E.Z.'s eyes got big. "Really? He can see me?"

"Of course he can see you, E.Z. You aren't a ghost."

His face got red. "Tell him, 'thank you, sir, I'm happy to meet you.'"

"He can hear you."

"Oh. Yeah. That's true." He gave a self-conscious laugh. "Where is he now?"

"Right there in that chair." She pointed at it. "That's his favorite place to sit."

"Hmphf!" Mr. Abernathy jerked on his jacket sleeves as he muttered, "I hardly have a choice, do I?"

"He's sorta stuck here in the kitchen," Charlotte explained to E.Z.

"That's tough. I'm sorry about that. But, dude, why'd you knock my cap off? That was lame."

"I assume he is speaking the current vernacular. Speech patterns of youth deliberately confound the adult brain," Mr. Abernathy said, casting a sharp glance at E.Z.'s rumpled brown hair. "Charlotte, tell this young man why I knocked his cap off his head."

"Mr. A believes in manners, and he says you should not wear a cap in the house."

"I didn't know that was like, y'know, a rule." He picked his cap up off the floor.

"Mr. Abernathy is very proper."

The man sniffed importantly and shifted in his chair.

"Thank you, my dear."

"So, since you can really see this guy, is he like a mist? Can you see right through him?"

"He looks as solid as you," Charlotte said. "That's why I wasn't completely sure he was a ghost at first. That's why the cop was here—because I called 9-1-1. I thought he was an intruder."

She decided not to mention the wind chimes. If she were to tell E.Z. about hearing them, she'd have to tell him about Janelle Dunmark and the others. She didn't want to talk about them, not now. Maybe never.

"So here's the thing," Charlotte said. "Mr. A says he was killed here in the kitchen."

E.Z.'s mouth flew open. "No way! For real?"

"For real. And he doesn't know who did it."

"That's rotten."

"So I'm going to find out for him."

"You are?"

She nodded. "I could use someone to help me. Would you like to do that?"

Charlotte had never seen him grin so big. "Sure. I'm doin' nothing else this summer."

"What's that?" Mr. Abernathy said, looking outraged. "A strapping young fellow like him isn't working? Why, he could be winnowing hay, or sweeping out the butcher shop."

"I don't think anyone does that anymore," Charlotte said to him. "Besides, don't you want him to help me? With two of us working on your case we could probably figure out your murderer's identity a lot quicker."

He pursed his mouth. "Well, I suppose you have a point."

"What? What's he saying?" E.Z. asked.

"He's wondering if you have a job."

"Sometimes I mow a couple of lawns on Saturdays. But Ma always takes my money as soon as I get paid. She says she'll buy groceries with it, but she usually buys cigarettes."

"That's totally unfair," she said.

"I know, right?"

"Tell that young man—"

"His name is E.Z."

"Tell E.Z. to open an account in the bank and deposit his money before his mother has a chance to take it from him. Cigarettes indeed!" He sniffed with annoyance.

She told E.Z. what Mr. Abernathy said. "Now, are you willing to help me solve Mr. Abernathy's murder?"

"Sure!"

"Then let's review the case. I'll get my notes and be right back. Here, Mr. A, take a look at this." She grabbed a book from her backpack and handed it over.

When she came back with her notes, an extra notebook and two pens, E.Z. was sitting at the table, gawking as Mr. Abernathy thumbed through the pages. For him, it would look as if the pages were turning all by themselves. She sat down and handed him a notebook and one of the pens.

"You aren't going to tell people about this, right?" she asked him.

"And have people think you're nuts? No way! Like you said, you keep my secret and I keep yours."

She nodded, and he lifted his fist for a bump.

"Deal!" they said together.

"Mr. A?" E.Z. held out his fist, and Mr. Abernathy frowned.

"C'mon," Charlotte coaxed the ghost. "We're a team. Fist bump to seal the deal."

"Must I? Is my word not good enough?"

Charlotte looked into his round eyes, her expression stern. She didn't say a word, just kept looking at him. He was going to have to learn to adapt to the modern world.

"Oh, well then." He huffed and puffed a bit, then made a pudgy fist. All three fists met on a gust of cold air.

CHAPTER
THIRTEEN

"**Y**ou need to take notes, E.Z.," Charlotte said, tapping the notebook and pen she'd given him.

He shoved them away. "I won't need that stuff."

"Sure you will." She pushed them back toward him. "Taking notes will help you think. Maybe you can come up with some good ideas."

He shook his head. "Nope. I can think just fine without help."

"Listen, E.Z., I'm not trying to be bossy or anything, but I plan to be an investigative journalist when I'm grown. My dad's a detective and he knows a lot about investigating. We've talked quite a bit about what to do when you're trying to find out stuff. This is my first story. If you don't want to be a part of it, that's okay. But if you want to help me, you have to cooperate. The only way we're going to learn who killed Mr. A. is to dig up every bit of information we can find."

"I'm more than happy to dig, but I'm not going to take notes." He moved the pen and notebook farther away.

She glared at him. "But you have to know all these facts about Mr. Abernathy and the people who were around him at that time."

"Tell me what I need to know. I have a good memory."

She huffed. "Listen, just read and copy what I've written. There isn't a lot there and it won't take you very long. Then, as you find out stuff, you can add—"

"I'm not taking any notes!" He stood. "If you expect me to read stuff and take notes, then I guess I'll not be a part of this."

She and Mr. Abernathy stared at his red face and flashing eyes.

"What's wrong with that boy?" Mr. Abernathy asked.

"I don't know. E.Z., why are you so angry?"

He glowered at her. "You know. You heard my granny."

She and Mr. Abernathy exchanged glances. "Your granny didn't say much worth hearing. What are you talking about?"

His jaw clenched and unclenched, and so did his hands.

"You know. You heard her say I can't read!"

Mr. Abernathy sniffed and shifted in his chair. "Doesn't he go to school? A young man his age should be educated if he wants to make something of himself!"

"You can't read ... at all?"

E.Z. made an impatient gesture. "The words are all scrambled on the page." He glared as if daring her to challenge him. "So, yeah, I can't read or take notes. I have a good memory, though. You tell me something once, and I remember it. But if that's not good enough to help with your case, I can just ... y'know, go home."

"Heavenly days!" Mr. Abernathy sighed. "What does he mean? Is he an imbecile?"

"No!" Charlotte said, nearly shouting at him. "He has a learning disability but that doesn't mean he's dumb." She patted E.Z.'s chair. "Sit down, and I'll read all this to you, then we'll discuss our next step."

He stared at her long and hard before his expression softened. "You don't think I'm too stupid to work with you?"

"You don't seem stupid to me."

"What about him?" He pointed in the general direction of Mr. Abernathy. "Did he just say I was dumb?"

"He doesn't know about dyslexia. We'll have to educate him." Mr. Abernathy jutted out his chin as if he was being insulted, but before he could say a word, Charlotte added, "Mr. Abernathy knows the benefit of being informed."

"You sure?"

"I'm sure."

E.Z. thought about it for another minute or so, then

nodded. "All right. Cool." He settled in his chair again. "Tell me about this case."

When Charlotte had finished reading all her notes, including the names she'd got from Mr. Abernathy and the questions her dad had told her to ask, he nodded.

"Got it!"

"You remember *all* the names of our suspects?" she asked.

"Sure. Minerva Van Elder, the housekeeper and cook; Emma Stamp the secretary, Jane Fillmore, the phone operator." He paused and gave Charlotte a puzzled look. "What's that?"

"The operator works the telephone switchboard in her office, answering calls and connecting people with one another." She slid a glance to Mr. Abernathy. "Right?"

"Right."

"Who else is on the list, E.Z.?" she asked.

"Catherine Anders, Mr. A's crush—"

"My what?" Mr. Abernathy looked very disturbed by this. "I've never crushed a woman in my life!"

"That just means you liked her, but she didn't know it," Charlotte explained.

His face relaxed, and he sat back in his chair.

E.Z. continued the list. "—and Horatio Ewing Lawson the Second."

"Excellent!" Mr. Abernathy said, nearly smiling. "In spite of his predilection for slang, the young man has a brain."

Charlotte grinned. "Mr. Abernathy totally approves. He thinks you're smart."

E.Z.'s smile spread all over his face. "Tell him thanks."

"Gosh, E.Z. Tell him yourself."

"Oh, yeah. I keep forgetting he can hear me. Thanks, Mr. A."

Mr. Abernathy blinked at him, then said, "Forget what I said about his having a brain. I think perhaps it only functions occasionally."

"He says 'you're welcome,'" Charlotte said to E.Z., who beamed in the general direction of the ghost.

"I said no such thing." Mr. Abernathy fiddled with his bow tie.

"So listen, none of these people are alive after all this time," she said. "We need to find their relatives. You've lived in Park City a long time, right?"

"All my life," E.Z. replied.

"Do you recognize any of the last names?"

"No, but granny might. She's older than Moses."

Charlotte thought about the old woman sitting in the chair, watching wrestling, calling E.Z. names then banishing him from the house.

"You think she'd tell us anything?"

He shrugged. "We can ask. But what does the ghost dude say about these people? Does he know where they are?"

She glanced at Mr. Abernathy. He shook his head. "I have told you everything I can remember, child."

"Mr. A, I bet you can remember a lot more than you realize if you try. Even a small clue might help us track down information."

"I'll try, but...." He spread his hands to indicate helplessness.

"The best anyone can do is to try."

He sighed, and a chill slid through the air.

E.Z. twirled his cap on his index finger, eyes narrowed in thought. Charlotte stared out the window. It was so quiet in the kitchen she could hear Mom's shears snipping through fabric upstairs.

"What about the Golden Sunset Manor?" E.Z. said.

Mr. Abernathy perked up like a wilted plant that had just been watered. He leaned forward, his gaze on the boy.

"What's the Golden Sunset Manor?" Charlotte asked.

"The nursing home on the other end of town. It's packed with really old people. Every time Granny swipes Ma's smokes, Ma threatens to take her there."

The more E.Z. talked about his home life, the more Charlotte was grateful for her own, even if it wasn't perfect.

"Charlotte," Mom called. "Honey, come up here and put on this dress so I can see how it flows when you walk."

Charlotte rolled her eyes and got up. "Uh oh. I might be gone for a while. E.Z., why don't you lay out the other library books for Mr. Abernathy to look at? Help yourself to some more food if you want."

"You got it," E.Z. said, reaching for the backpack.

She pinned a look on the ghost. "Mr. A, I hope you'll be nice to E.Z."

Mr. Abernathy sniffed as if she had offended him. "I fail to appreciate a child admonishing her elders. At any rate, I am always nice to others."

Charlotte glanced over her shoulder as she went through the kitchen door.

"So, dude, here's what Charlotte thought you might like. And she didn't get anything trashy." E.Z. placed the books in front of Mr. Abernathy as if he could see the ghost as well as he could see the chair in which the man sat.

CHAPTER
FOURTEEN

The next morning, E.Z. was sitting on the front stoop when Charlotte stepped outside to get the newspaper.

"Oh!" she said, jumping a little.

"Sorry. I didn't mean to scare you."

"You didn't scare me. You startled me. I don't get scared."

"Uh huh." He smiled with his eyes. "Well, then, I didn't mean to startle you, but I thought you might want to get busy on our investigation today."

She plucked up the newspaper from off the grass and brushed away a tiny ant that was running along the length of it.

"I want breakfast before I do any work. It helps me to think. Have you eaten?"

He looked away. "I had a pop."

"That's not breakfast. You like Lucky Charms? Or

we got Cornflakes. Mom likes bran nuggets. I can't stand bran nuggets, but we have a big box of 'em."

"I like any of it."

"C'mon in the house, and we'll discuss our strategy over breakfast."

"Nah, I'll wait for you out here."

She gave him a puzzled look. "Why?"

"I had supper here last night, and lunch yesterday."

"So?"

"Well, I mean…well…." He spun the wheels on his skateboard.

"Come on. We have a lot to do."

He hesitated a moment longer. "Well, okay, then. Hang on. I'll be back in a second."

He leaned the skateboard against the steps, dashed across the street and into his house. He emerged a minute later, shutting the door on his grandmother's screeching voice. He trotted across the street, carrying a sack.

"I brought some stuff for you and your mom."

"You don't have to give us anything."

"I want to." An eager, happy look burned in his eyes. To refuse would hurt his pride and his feelings.

She smiled. "Thanks, E.Z."

In the kitchen he pulled out four cans of Pepsi, two cans of SpaghettiOs, a can of green beans, and can of tuna packed in water. She thought of how empty the kitchen seemed in his house. The offering touched Charlotte, and she felt a rush of warmth toward her friend.

"Are you sure about this, E.Z.?"

"I'm sure."

She glanced at Mr. Abernathy. He was nodding, gesturing for her to accept E.Z.'s gift.

"Thank you, E.Z. We can have SpaghettiOs for lunch."

"Sure." He grinned. "And lookit." He pulled out a large manila envelope that was sealed. "The school sent this to Ma a long time ago. It's about dyslexia and other learning disorders and stuff, I guess. I thought Mr. A might want to read it, so he can know I'm not stupid and that I don't have, like, a disease or something."

"Will your mom care?"

"Nah. She never even opened it. Let Mr. A have it."

"You're a good guy, E.Z."

She opened the envelope and handed the contents to Mr. Abernathy who thanked her profusely.

"Let's go to the Clairmonte Hotel and see what we can find there," Charlotte suggested as they ate breakfast.

E.Z. had his mouth full, so he nodded and gave her a thumbs-up.

"That's capital!" Mr. Abernathy said, beaming at them. His face took on a dreamy expression, and he half-closed his eyes. "The marble floors, the chandeliers that sparkle like ice…oh, the beautiful, manicured grounds with exotic shrubs trimmed to perfection. And the fountain, the splashing crystal water. The Clairmonte, a true work of art, one of a kind in Park City."

Charlotte and E.Z. exchanged a quick look. How would they ever be able to tell him the sorry, sad shape it was in now?

"What should we take with us?" E.Z. asked.

"I'll take a pen and notebook. You bring your amazing memory. What about snacks? Think we ought to pack a lunch?"

"We can take the SpaghettiOs and a couple of spoons."

The mere thought of cold SpaghettiOs from the can made Charlotte's stomach lurch. "How about if I fix us some sandwiches, and we have the SpaghettiOs here tomorrow?"

"The Clairmonte offers excellent luncheon," Mr. Abernathy put in. "You should try—"

Mom walked into the kitchen, and he snapped his lips shut as if she could hear him.

"Good morning, Charlotte. Did you make coffee yet? I brought the coffee pot back in here, didn't I?" She glanced around the room, her gaze falling on the boy. "Why, good morning, E.Z. I didn't know you were here."

"Good mornin', ma'am." His smile was uncertain, and he looked skittish, as if he thought she might send him back home again.

"There's coffee, Mom," Charlotte said. "I brought the pot down yesterday and made you some the minute I got up."

"Thank you, honey." She poured coffee then spotted

the cans he had brought. "What's that? Where did those SpaghettiOs come from, Charlotte? I didn't know you still liked them."

"E.Z. brought them. I told him he didn't have to do that."

"But I want to," he said quickly. "It's the right thing to do."

Mom smiled at him. "Thank you, honey. You and Charlotte can enjoy them for lunch. I'm making meatloaf and mashed potatoes tonight." She blew on her coffee to cool it. "So what are you two going to do today?"

Charlotte figured if Mom knew they were going to that awful old hotel, she'd immediately envision it collapsing on top of them and would forbid them from going.

"E.Z. is going to show me around town."

"Oh?" Mom leaned against the counter and sipped her coffee. "I suppose there are some interesting things to see in Park City."

"Well, there's the park. And the fire station. And the school. There's the Wham Burger. And the oldest church in the county isn't far away. It's made completely from rocks. They call it Rock Church."

"There are plenty of rocks in the Ozarks to build things out of," Mom said with a laugh.

"That's for sure," E.Z. agreed.

"The church!" Mr. Abernathy shouted. "I forgot about the church. I think I'm buried in the church cemetery."

Charlotte shot him a startled glance.

"In fact," he continued, "there is a records book and a huge Bible on a special stand in the vestibule. It holds records of births, marriages, and deaths. And the causes of deaths."

"We have to see the church then!" Charlotte said.

"Excellent!"

"Okay," E.Z. said. "I can show it to you."

"You know what?" Mom said, thoughtfully, a dreamy look on her face, "I should go with you two. I've hardly been out of this house, and I really do need to know more about this town."

E.Z. and Charlotte exchanged looks.

"But what about your work?" Charlotte asked. The last thing she needed was Mom coming along while they were doing their investigations.

Mom clunked the coffee cup down on the countertop. "I need a break from work. You kids wait for me while I run up and take a shower, then we'll go look at some of the sights. And then we'll go to Wham Burger for lunch."

"Wham Burger? Really? That's my favorite!" E.Z.'s hazel eyes sparkled. As soon as she was upstairs, he asked Charlotte, "She doesn't know about the ghost dude, right?"

"My name is Clarence Albert Abernathy." He scowled and fiddled with his bow tie.

"I think you should call him Mr. Abernathy, not the ghost dude," Charlotte said. "And no, my mom doesn't know anything about him so don't mention him, please. Listen, we can look around for ideas then go on our own later."

"All right. If we go to the cemetery behind the church, you can look for names, and I'll look for dates."

"You aren't dyslexic about numbers?"

"Not much. Just if I'm tired or sick, they jump around on the page, but not as bad as letters."

Mom came into the room a few minutes later with her hair still wet from the shower. "Okay, kids, I'm ready to go."

Charlotte's mother was lovely, but she never took much interest in her appearance, especially when she was working. Charlotte always thought it was odd that someone who loved fashion as much as Jennifer Franklin did went around in mismatched, wrinkled clothes and her hair sticking out every which way, not caring a bit about how she looked. Dad always said that her appearance and distracted state of mind were the signs that the artist inside her was awake and working.

That day, though, she was dressed neatly in khaki capris, white blouse, and sandals. She looked casual, comfortable, and pretty. Normal.

With Charlotte in the backseat and E.Z. in the front passenger seat, Mom drove through Park City. E.Z. pointed out different buildings and landmarks, telling what was special about them.

"If you turn right on the next street, you'll see the Sage County courthouse. It's older'n dirt."

They drove slowly past a square brick building three stories tall with a clock tower and surrounded by huge maple trees.

"It's charming," Mom said. "Look at that nineteenth century architecture."

Charlotte eyed the place carefully, knowing a lot of information was stored in courthouses. She didn't care about architecture or age, just as long as it had information she might need. She had left her notebook back home, figuring with Mom along, she and E.Z. wouldn't be able to do much investigating or note-taking.

They turned down another tree-lined street with older, well-kept homes. Every one of those houses had big front porches and lots of flower beds.

"There's Rock Church," E.Z. said.

The church was a tall, narrow structure. It sat back from the street with two large oak trees growing on either side. Five broad concrete steps led up to a porch and double wooden doors.

"Isn't it lovely?" Mom sighed as she parked.

As soon as they got out, Charlotte and E.Z. ran to the building and up the steps. She trailed her fingers along the sun-warmed, rough stones. From a distance, the rocks looked rusty brown, but up close she saw each one was different, some smooth and gray, others rough and striped red and dark yellow.

"This is awesome," E.Z. said. "I've been past this place a million times and never really looked at it."

Mom was taking photos with the phone and murmuring to herself.

"She's getting new ideas," Charlotte said. "Stuff like this gives her brain a kick."

Charlotte read the polished brass plaque by the front door. "Rock Church, Founded 1889 by Francis Bonnet, Horatio Ewing Lawson, and Ansel Gracen."

"Horatio Ewing Lawson," E.Z. said. "That's one of the names on your list."

"Yep. But the name on our list is Horatio Ewing Lawson, the second."

"Then this church dude is probably that dude's old man."

"Probably so." She tried the doors and found them locked. "I'd sure like to go inside. Mr. A said there's a records book with births and deaths in it and a great big Bible on a special stand in the church vestibule."

"What's a vestibule?"

"An entry, like a foyer."

"But that was a long time ago, Charlotte. You think it would still be there?"

"I don't know, but churches keep stuff like that for a long time. It would be historical and special, so maybe it is."

"Good point," he said, nodding.

"Plus, Mr. A thinks he was buried in the cemetery here."

"Oh, yeah? The cemetery is behind the church. Let's go look for his grave, want to?"

"Let's go see." Mom was still taking photos. "Hey, Mom. E.Z. and I are going to look at the graveyard, okay?"

"Sure, honey. Don't get hurt."

Charlotte could tell by the dreamy, absent tone in Mom's voice that the reply was automatic. Her mother probably didn't even know she'd spoken. The fact that Mom was such a worrier but could space out as if she lived on another planet was something that made Chloe and Olivia call her weird.

The back of the building was plain, with two windows and a stoop leading to the backdoor. A bright white picket fence enclosed rows of gravestones in a neatly-mown cemetery. Charlotte wondered if the fence was to keep people out...or to keep them in. The idea creeped her out a little and she pushed it away from her thoughts.

She heard the faint, soft sound of wind chimes. Or maybe she just imagined it.

"Hey! Look at this." E.Z. shook the doorknob of the old wooden backdoor. "We can get in, real easy. One of Ma's boyfriends showed me how. Your mom would have a ring-tailed fit if we went inside, huh?"

Right then, as distracted as Mom was with taking photos, Charlotte doubted the woman would notice if everyone in the graveyard climbed out of their coffins and started to sing. But the cold hand of reason tapped Charlotte on the shoulder. Breaking and entering could get them both into serious trouble.

On the other hand, how else would they get into the church to look at that records book Mr. Abernathy mentioned?

"Charlotte? E.Z.?" Mom called. "Where'd you kids run off to?" Her voice grew closer. E.Z. leaped off the stoop and joined Charlotte by the white fence.

"Back here," Charlotte replied.

Her mom came around the corner, a worried expression on her face. "Why are you two back here by the cemetery?"

Charlotte sighed. It was typical of her absent-minded mother to have forgotten what Charlotte told her a couple of minutes earlier.

"There are some cool gravestones in there," E.Z. said. "You might get some more ideas for your designs."

"Oh?" Her gaze trailed slowly over the stones. She fingered her necklace. "Perhaps you're right. Let's go look. But you kids be careful. Don't get hurt."

E.Z. and Charlotte followed her through the gate. Charlotte looked carefully at every name. From time to time, she found stones with quotes on them and read them aloud for E.Z. "In the arms of Jesus." "Gone, but not forgotten." "Singing in the heavenly choir."

"Oh, my goodness!" Mom said. She stood several rows away, staring at a tall monument Charlotte and E.Z. had not yet reached.

"What is it?" Charlotte asked as they hurried toward her.

"That." She pointed at the grave marker. "It's our house!"

161

CHAPTER FIFTEEN

Charlotte read the name carved into the stone and exclaimed, "It's Mr. Abernathy's grave!"

Mom was taking pictures with her phone. "Who?"

"The man who built our house."

"How do you know that, honey?"

Charlotte met E.Z.'s eyes silently asking him to say nothing. "There's some town history at the library."

"How interesting that his tombstone looks like the house." Her mom took more photos up close.

"I bet that would make him happy," Charlotte said. "If he knew, I mean."

Mom turned a speculative gaze on her and held it so long, Charlotte felt like she was trying to read her mind. "Why would you say that?"

She was glad her mom couldn't hear the insistent ringing of wind chimes that grew slowly and steadily louder. That meant somebody was nearby, many somebodies, maybe. They were, after all, in a cemetery.

"Charlotte Franklin," her mom said, frowning. "None of this Janelle Dunmark business, and I mean it."

"Mom."

"I mean it. I won't have it."

E.Z.'s glance passed back and forth between them. As if he recognized Charlotte's need to escape from the conversation, he spoke up.

"Hey look! Over there is another tombstone house." He jogged toward it and Charlotte followed, grateful to get away from Mom's hard stare.

"What's the name on that one?" he asked when they reached it.

"It's Horatio's."

"The dad or the dude?"

"The dude."

"Whoa. Weird how he and Mr. A have the same kind of marker, huh?"

"It is."

They fell silent as Mom approached. "Do you recognize that house, E.Z.?" she asked.

"No, ma'am. But maybe it's on the other side of town, or burned down, or something."

"Look at that marker over there, Mom. Look at all the squiggles and flowers carved into it."

Mom followed Charlotte's gaze. "That's a Celtic symbol. Irish and Scottish and the like. Isn't it lovely?"

Just as Charlotte had hoped, Mom's focus turned from Janelle Dunmark and Charlotte to something existing in her own mind. The longer she studied the intricate design, the more she turned inward. When she got like this, Charlotte knew it was only a matter of time until Mom was completely lost in her own thoughts again.

She and E.Z. continued to stroll through the cemetery, but Charlotte kept one eye on her mother. From the corner of her eye, she saw movement along the edge of the cemetery. She knew at least one spirit stood there, waiting to be acknowledged. Mr. Abernathy was enough for her to deal with. She didn't want any more ghosts talking to her. If she didn't look at the person directly, maybe they'd just go away and stop staring at her.

"It's time to go home now." Mom said after a time. She turned and walked toward the gate.

Charlotte was relieved, but E.Z. wore a look of disappointment. She was pretty sure she knew why.

"Mom, you promised us lunch at Wham Burger, remember?"

"Hmm?" She might as well have been on the moon.

"You promised us lunch at Wham Burger. Remember?"

"Did I?"

She opened the gate and indicated for them to precede her. She stood with her hand on the gate latch for a moment, gazing at them as if trying to figure out who they were.

"Well, of course I did," she said with a self-conscious laugh. "I remember now. But I must sketch these design ideas before I lose them. How about if I drop you off, and you walk home? Or is it too far? Is it on a busy highway? Because I absolutely forbid you to walk on a busy highway."

"I know the back way from the Wham Burger, ma'am," E.Z. said quickly. "It's through a nice quiet neighborhood, and we can cut across that way."

"Oh?" Her mom gave him a doubtful look and rubbed the tip of her finger over the gold circlet at her throat.

"I only go where it's safe, ma'am, and I'd never let Charlotte get hurt."

She hesitated a moment longer. "You're sure it's safe?"

"I'm one hundred percent positive."

"All right, then. But you must promise me, both of you, that you'll be careful."

"We will," they said in unison.

When she dropped them off at the Wham Burger, she handed Charlotte some money and the cell phone.

"Take this. Use the phone only for an emergency. Bring me back the change. And be careful walking home."

"Your mom might be a little forgetful," E.Z. said as she drove away, "but she's awesome. My ma would never, in a thousand years, give me money for Wham Burger."

"Mom's all right," Charlotte agreed. She held up the

phone. "The notebook is back at the house, so I can't take notes, but at least we can take pictures."

"Hey, I'm better than any ol' notebook. Just tell me what you need to remember and I'll remember it for you. C'mon. Let's go eat. I'm starvin'."

Later, after they'd polished off their lunch and disposed of the cups and wrappers, he said, "The Clairmonte isn't far from here. You wanna go see what we can find out there?"

"Yes!"

The Clairmonte Hotel stood back from the street a few yards. The broken pavement of the driveway made a semi-circle, leading cars to the front door and leading back to the street. Weeds sprouted in the cracks and crowded the edges of the driveway. The lawn must have been pretty at one time, but on that day, it was ragged and patchy, full of overgrown dandelions.

"I've never been this close to it before." E.Z. said as they walked up the driveway.

Charlotte grimaced as she eyed the place. "It doesn't look anything like what Mr. Abernathy said."

"Yeah, it's really rundown."

"Let's not tell Mr. A how bad it looks. It would just make him feel bad."

"Okay." E.Z. stopped and pointed at the peak in the center. "Do you know what those monsters are called?"

Charlotte used her hand to shade her eyes and

squinted. Squat figures with fearsome faces glowered out at the world.

"Those are gargoyles."

"Cool. Like that movie *Gargoyles on 13th Street*?"

"I doubt it. I read once that gargoyles are supposed to protect from evil spirits."

He turned a surprised expression on her. "I thought they ate bones. Y'know, people bones. They did in the movie."

She waved one hand. "That's a dumb movie, then. C'mon, let's see what it's like inside. Maybe someone in there can tell us why this place is such a wreck."

The front door came unstuck with a loud shudder when they both pulled on it. They nearly stumbled into a tall room that echoed the sound of the door when it slammed shut behind them.

Inside, it was cool and dim, but the first thing Charlotte noticed was the stink. It reminded her of the sour musty odor of E.Z.'s house, only about one hundred times worse. The marble walls and floor had probably been a pretty gray and white along time ago, but now they looked streaked and stained, as if they emitted the stench.

A thin, bald man in an undershirt with a blue tattoo of an anchor on his arm looked up from behind a high desk and gave them a flinty once-over. His face looked as yellowed and mottled as the marble.

"What're you kids doin' in here?" His voice bounced off the walls.

"I wish I had my notebook!" Charlotte muttered. "We'd look more professional if we had notebooks."

"Two kids in T-shirts and shorts don't look professional, with or without notebooks," E.Z. said. "And don't worry. I'm gonna remember everything."

The bald man came out from behind the desk. He was shriveled, with a sallow face as wrinkled as a dried apple. His red and blue plaid shorts were a size or two too big for him. Charlotte almost giggled when she saw he wore brown socks with his sandals.

"What're you doin' in here? This ain't no place for ankle-biters."

"We're not ankle-biters," Charlotte said. "We'd like to talk to someone."

He pinned his gaze on her. "Well? Talk!"

"We're looking for some information about this old hotel," E.Z. said.

"Elmo," someone shouted from the steps leading upstairs. "We don't got no more toilet paper."

Elmo waved one arm at the speaker, as though chasing off something annoying.

"What possible interest could you have in this dump?" he asked.

"We'd like to know when and why it went from being the nicest place in town to…well, this." Charlotte gestured around her.

He grunted like something caused him pain. "Look. I don't know anything about that. I just work here. And none of these jokers know anything either." He walked up to them so close Charlotte smelled his sweat. She worked hard not to wrinkle her nose. "Listen to me." His voice was really quiet. "Some of these people in here is fresh outta jail, or they're tanked up. Some of 'em is high on the dope. This ain't no place for kids, so y'uns go on and get out and don't never come back."

Charlotte refused to give up so easily. "All we want to know if you know something about Clarence Albert Abernathy who once owned the Clairmonte."

Irritation settled deeper into his wrinkles. "Never heard of 'im."

"May we talk to the owner?"

"I reckon you could, if you lived in Atlanta, Georgia, cuz that's where the company is who bought this place. But they own about hundred other run-down places like this and likely they don't know nothin', either."

Charlotte's heart sank.

"Maybe you have some papers or something in the basement or somewhere?" E.Z. suggested.

"Kid, that basement has been flooded so many times if there was ever any paperwork down there, it'd be rotten by now. Nothing down there but rats and cockroaches."

"Are you sure—"

"Listen. I've done run out of patience. Y'uns got to the count of five then I'm gonna call the law to come and take you home."

Charlotte knew he'd do it, too. He was just that

cranky. If a policeman took her home, no telling what Mom would do. Have a cow, probably.

"Well, that was a big fat waste of time," she said when they were outside. "And I don't think I'll ever get that stink out of my nose."

"Yeah, that was rank. Maybe walking in the fresh air will get the smell off of us."

"I hope so. Ew, ew, ew." She shook herself trying to shake off the odor.

E.Z. stretched as if the Clairmonte had twisted his muscles and bones. "So you wanna go back to Rock Church?"

"There's no point. We can't get in, remember."

"Yeah, but we can look around. Maybe we can peek in the windows or something. Maybe we can see into the vestibule from a window and see if the stand that held the book and the Bible is still there."

She thought about this. If she was going to live a life of an investigator, she had to learn to take what opportunities she could find. Looking in windows was a tiny opportunity, but it was worth a shot.

"Let's go," she said.

CHAPTER SIXTEEN

"That church is the most awesome building I've seen in Park City," Charlotte said as it came into view.

They walked faster, eager to reach their destination and start investigating. Charlotte ignored the wind chimes that started as soon as they stepped onto church property.

"Let's see if we can peek in any windows," she said.

They walked around the church, but every window was too high off the ground, even for E.Z., who was taller than her by a few inches. They went to the front doors and tried to peek through the tiny crack between them but saw nothing.

E.Z. pointed to the small, screened grates, almost like windows, beneath the building. "Those are to let air circulate under the church. I betcha there's a basement or a crawl space."

Before she could reply, he lay flat on the ground next to one of the grates, his face pressed against it.

"Can't see a thing." He got up and brushed himself off. "Dark as the inside of a cow."

"I guess we might as well go home," Charlotte said. She felt deflated.

"Not yet." E.Z. sprinted to the back of the church and she followed him. He went up the stoop to the back door and took a sheathed knife from the front pocket of his shorts.

"Do you always carry that?"

"Pretty much all the time. Well, not at school. If I took it to school, they'd take it away from me. The handle is made from a deer horn, and it's the only thing of my grandpa's that I have. He made it when he was about my age."

"You have a grandpa?"

"Yeah. Well, I did. Granny's old man. He died a few years ago." He opened the knife to expose a thin blade. "Listen, Charlotte, you better not watch how I do this."

She frowned. "Why not? Is this some kind of 'girls shouldn't know this stuff?' or 'girls shouldn't touch knives?'"

"No. But if you don't know how to do this, and we get caught or something, you won't be the one to get in big trouble."

"If we get caught, we'll both be in trouble. Besides, investigative reporters have to go where they aren't supposed to, all the time. This is good experience."

"That's true."

He slid a sideways glance at her, then snapped his head up, frowning at something behind her. "What in the world is *that*? Over there on the other side of the cemetery! Do you see it?"

Without pausing to think, she turned and looked. Surely E.Z. didn't see spirits, did he? She saw nothing.

"Hey! We're in," he announced.

She spun around, saw the open door, and realized what he'd done. "That was a sneaky trick, E.Z."

He merely grinned and indicated for her to enter. Her stomach knotted, and she knew this was a risk. But she refused to let poor Mr. Abernathy stay stuck in the kitchen for another hundred years. If she could help him by finding out what happened, she'd take the risk. Besides, they would only be inside the church long enough to find the records book and look inside it for information.

They walked into a mudroom with hooks on the walls for coats and scarves. There was a small shelf with cleaning supplies. Swept clean and perfectly tidy, it ran the width of the church. Four steps led up to a door. Charlotte ascended them and turned the knob.

She and E.Z. walked into the sanctuary. It had pure white walls and shining oak floors and pews. The clear-paned windows sparkled, letting hot summer sunshine pour inside. The silence in that large room was deep and pure, as if nothing outside could ever disturb its peace.

"Awesome!" E.Z. said in a quiet voice.

"It's beautiful."

"Those benches have purple cushions on them." He fell silent for a moment. "Look, Charlotte! It's a grand piano." He walked toward a black piano that shone as brightly as mirrors.

"It's baby grand," she said. "A grand piano would take up this whole stage. Come on, E.Z. Let's find that records book."

"But—"

"You can look at the piano afterward."

He hesitated, casting a look of longing at the piano, then followed her to the back of the sanctuary. Just beyond was the vestibule—a small square room where people entered the church. On the far side of that room were the two large wooden doors that led out onto the church's big front porch.

A table in the vestibule stood on one side. It held leaflets, flyers, and a couple of Bibles. There was no special stand with a records book or Bible. Charlotte huffed with disappointment.

"Not much in here," E.Z. said.

Her glance fell on a closed door on the far wall. She opened it and found a room crowded with a large desk and bulging-full bookshelves.

"Maybe that book Mr. Abernathy mentioned is somewhere on these shelves."

She glanced at E.Z. He was gazing at the row after row of books, his expression confused, even pained. It must be terrible to see the titles and author names and have no idea what they said.

"The records book will be really old, so just look for old books," she told him. "Any old book. Don't worry about the title."

The room was small and crowded, and the air conditioner had probably been shut off after services on Sunday, so it was also broiling hot. By the time they had searched every shelf, not only had they found no records book, but they were also drenched with sweat.

Charlotte stared at the desk, her conscience prickling with warning at the thought of searching through it. But they'd already broken into a church. How could it matter now if she looked in the desk drawers for anything about Mr. Abernathy?

She opened the top drawer and found nothing but supplies like rubber bands, pens, and a stapler.

"I'll look in all the drawers on this side so we can get through before we melt into two greasy puddles," E.Z. said.

"Good idea."

With both of them searching, they completed the task quickly but found nothing helpful. Charlotte hoped no one would ever know she had been in this room and rummaging through this desk. She reminded herself again that this is what some reporters have to do if they want a story. Even her dad, the detective, had to pry and prowl in places he normally wouldn't. She doubted he felt guilty about it. It was simply something that had to be done.

She closed the office door softly, as if someone might hear the snick of the latch.

"I saw steps in that mudroom that probably leads into a basement," E.Z. said. "Shouldn't we look down there?"

"For sure. Maybe they've stored old records in it."

As they made their way back to the front of the church, E.Z. gave the piano such a look of longing over his shoulder that her heart twisted. He had so little in his life and seemed so grateful for even the smallest, briefest of good things.

"You're really interested in that piano, huh?" she asked.

"Yeah. I've never really seen one up close."

"Do you play any instruments?"

"Nope. I wanted to take band, but Ma said we couldn't afford to rent an instrument, and Granny said the noise would drive her nuts, so...." He shrugged.

"Then while I investigate downstairs, why don't you take a look at that piano?"

His eyes lit up. "Really?"

"How many times are you going to have a chance to examine a baby grand?" Still he hesitated. She smiled and gave him a gentle push toward the piano. "Go on now."

"All right then!" He started toward it but stopped and looked back at her with a big smile that reached his eyes. "You're really awesome, Charlotte."

Her face turned warm. "Thanks, E.Z. So are you."

Looking down the steep, narrow staircase to the basement was like gazing into a dark pit. She felt along the wall for a light switch and found one. A bare bulb shone with a dull, yellowish glare. Cautiously, Charlotte descended the steps into a damp, murky basement with a dirt floor.

She did not like the dank odor that rose to meet her. Nor did she like the dark, dusty shadows that seemed to lurk everywhere. Very little light from the single bulb above the steps seeped into the corners. She hoped none of the residents of the cemetery outside waited for her down there.

She paused at the foot of the steps. Nearby sat three large plastic storage bins. Inside she found strings of Christmas lights, tinsel, red and green glass balls, fake holly and ivy, and plenty of other Christmas decorations. But no books, old or new. She heaved a sigh and moved away.

"I wish I had a flashlight," she muttered and walked straight into a cobweb hanging from the low ceiling. She shuddered, clenched her teeth, and scraped the clingy thing off her face and neck. She strained her eyes, trying to find another light switch. She walked into something other than cobwebs that dangled from the ceiling. It was a cord and she yanked it, hoping it was attached to a light. Sure enough, another bulb came on, chasing away some of her uneasiness. All she saw was an old bicycle, a galvanized washtub, and two large, ancient fans with big metal blades.

From upstairs a few random piano notes, lovely and sweet, drifted down. Then she heard a tune, "Mary Had a Little Lamb" being plunked out slowly. Just a few bars of that, then something else. Halting and slow at first, it was a familiar tune she'd heard on the radio. It picked up tempo and chords.

"Awesome!" E.Z. shouted. "Charlotte!"

She had seen everything that was to be found in the stinky, damp basement and quickly went back upstairs. E.Z.'s face was a study of happiness and amazement as he watched his fingers on the keyboard.

"I didn't know you could play the piano."

He looked up. "Neither did I. I just…it's like my fingers just know where to go. It's awesome! There's actually something I can do."

"You're great, E.Z. I know that song you were just playing. I've heard it a lot."

He grinned, then stopped playing to ask, "What did you do, crawl around on your belly in the basement?" He peered at the top of her head. "What's that?"

She reached up, plucked something brittle out of her hair and looked at it.

"Ugh. A dried-up spider. Gross." She flicked it away.

"Did you find anything—"

Without warning, the double doors in the vestibule flew open and two police officers, weapons drawn, charged into the church.

Faces grim, they approached, their guns pointed

right at Charlotte and E.Z.

"You kids! Get your hands up and don't move!"

CHAPTER
SEVENTEEN

Charlotte hated the ride to the police station in the backseat of the cruiser. It smelled like puke, pee, and other gross things. E.Z.'s frequent, "I'm so sorry" made her want to cry. Even worse was riding home from the police station later in Mom's car. Her mother's face was a mask of fury.

"What were you thinking?" she asked at least ten times. "Do you want a police record? Do you know what kind of people are in a jail? Do you know what could have happened to you? To you both!"

She glowered at E.Z. every bit as much as she glared at Charlotte.

"Yes, ma'am," they both said meekly every time.

She herded them into the house through the back door and pointed toward the kitchen table.

"Sit."

They sat. Only once did they risk looking at each

other and that was when Mom turned away long enough to get a drink of water.

"Well, well," Mr. Abernathy said, shifting a bit in his chair. "What has transpired to bring about this air of disquiet amongst the three of you? Why, your mother looks as if she might swoon."

Why did he persist in asking her questions in front of Mom?

"Mom, we didn't hurt anything inside that church—"

Mom whirled around. Mr. Abernathy was right. She looked like she might pass out, or maybe explode. Her pale blue eyes, usually dreamy and soft, glittered like ice.

"You were trespassing, Charlotte. You broke in! I will never, in a thousand years, understand why you broke into that church."

"Ma'am," E.Z. said. "Um, ma'am, Charlotte didn't break in. I did."

She glared at him. "You both did! The doors were locked, but you went inside."

"Yes, ma'am, but we didn't take anything, or break anything, or—"

"Enough!" she shouted, holding up both hands. Then, visibly trying to calm herself, she took a deep breath, closed her eyes, and pressed her fingertips against her temples for the count of twenty.

She opened her eyes and said, "Give me the cell phone, Charlotte." She held out one hand, palm up, beckoning with her fingers. "Hand it over. I'm going to call your father."

Charlotte dug the phone out of her pocket. Mom snatched it from her as if she thought Charlotte wouldn't let it go. She stomped off upstairs, saying as she went, "Do not move. Do not go anywhere."

"Am I given to understand you went into the Rock Church?" Mr. Abernathy said. He rested his hands on the table, fingertips touching.

"Yes, sir. We did."

"Surely the door wasn't locked, was it?"

"It was locked."

"A church with a locked door. Tsk, tsk."

"E.Z. knew how to…um…open the door."

"Indeed?" His gaze shifted to E.Z. who was jiggling his leg and tapping the table.

"Geez, I'm sorry, Charlotte. I'm real sorry."

"Please, stop saying that, E.Z. It was my idea." To Mr. Abernathy, she said, "We found your grave."

The disapproval fled from his expression, replaced with extreme interest. "Indeed?"

"Tell him we took pictures of it," E.Z. said, offering a quick, nervous smile in the direction of the ghost.

"He can hear you," Charlotte reminded him, patting his hand. "The pictures are on the phone, so I can't show them to you now, Mr. A."

"On the phone? But I thought…." Mr. Abernathy shook his head. "Ah, well. I know new-fangled gadgets are all the rage and always have been."

E.Z. looked so upset that Charlotte didn't know how to comfort him. She got some chips from the cabinet and

185

poured him a glass of cold sweet tea. When he shook his head, she got worried. E.Z. never refused food.

Mom's footsteps thundered down the stairs, and she came into the kitchen. Her lips and nostrils were pinched so tight Charlotte wondered how she could breathe. With her arms folded across her chest, Mom paced back and forth, hard, quick steps.

"Ma'am?" E.Z. said so quietly Charlotte could barely hear him.

Her mom whirled and pointed at him. "You. Right now, go home. Do not return. Not today, tonight, tomorrow, or next week. Perhaps never. You and Charlotte are no longer allowed to spend time together."

Charlotte's stomach tied in a hard knot. "Mom! You can't do—"

Her mother held up one hand, her jaw clenched.

E.Z.'s eyes filled with hurt, though he lifted his chin and straightened his shoulders. He was used to being kicked out of his own house.

"Mom, you don't understand. We—"

"I understand perfectly well, Coco Charlotte Franklin. You go up to your room and stay there until your father gets here. We'll see what he has to say about this!" She turned to E.Z. who stood still as a stone. "You, E.Z. Go home and tell your mother what happened."

"Ma isn't home. She's probably at Honey-B's, or maybe over at Tim's Grill."

Mom frowned. "At this time of day? Well, is your father home?"

His face turned dark red, and he shook his head. "No, ma'am."

Charlotte had told Mom that E.Z. didn't have a dad, but naturally she'd forgotten. Or maybe she hadn't heard in the first place. Charlotte loved Mom very much, but at that moment, she had a hard time liking her.

"Then no one is at your house?"

"Just Granny."

"Mom, wait a minute," Charlotte said. "You don't understand."

Her mom pointed at the door, her hand trembling. Why couldn't she stop being mad long enough to listen?

"Then go tell Granny," she ordered. "And remember what I said. Charlotte is no longer allowed to spend time with you, and you are not to come here."

"Yes, ma'am. I understand."

E.Z. went to the door. He put his hand on the knob, looked over his shoulder at Charlotte. "I'm sorry, Charlotte. I'm real, *real* sorry."

She wanted to say she was far sorrier than he was. She was so sorry that she wished she'd been born to a different mother. But words seemed stuck in her throat along with more anger than she had ever felt in her life.

As soon as E.Z. left, she slammed a hard look at her furious mom and went upstairs. She closed the door of her tiny room. Without the coolness from the small air conditioner in Mom's studio, the room would soon be hot and airless. Charlotte didn't care. It matched her mood.

She opened her window as wide as it would go, then flopped down on the bed. As upset as she was about Mom's stubborn refusal to listen, she felt ten times worse about E.Z. When she heard the wheels of a skateboard on the sidewalk, she scooted off the bed and looked out the window.

E.Z. was skating away, going toward town.

"I should go with him," she muttered.

She pressed her forehead against the thin, sun-warmed glass of her window. The ground was too far away for her to jump without breaking a bone or two. She rested her gaze on the big magnolia tree that shaded that side of the house. Were any of those thick branches close enough she could climb out the window, grab one, then shinny down?

No, of course not.

The rusty screen below the glass pane bulged outward, as if others had thought to escape the same way. Charlotte pricked her fingers on the sharp, brittle metal of the old screen as she tried to free it from the window, but it was nailed to the sill from the outside.

With a huff, she sat down on the edge of the bed and glared at the floor until she heard Mom moving around in the sewing studio.

She went to her door and opened it. "Mom, you don't understand what happened."

"Did I say you could come out of your room?"

"I'm in my room. But let me tell—"

Her mother stood in the doorway of her studio. Like

two angry bulldogs, they stared at each other across the length of the upstairs hallway.

"Nothing you can say will alter the fact that you and that boy broke into a church. Breaking and entering is against the law, Charlotte. It's a *crime*. And a church, of all places!"

"I wish you'd just listen—"

"I am not listening to a thing you have to say right now. There is nothing you can say that will make a bit of difference."

Charlotte wanted to scream, to jump up and down, beat her chest like a gorilla and pull out her own hair. But temper tantrums made everything worse. Not that being calm and trying to explain anything helped, either. Obviously. Mom had made up her mind, and that was that.

She closed her door and sat on the edge of the bed. She thought of Mr. Abernathy sitting in the kitchen. Charlotte opened her door again.

"May I at least go get something to eat and drink?"

Mom was in the studio, and she didn't answer right away. Was she thinking whether Charlotte should be allowed to have food and water? Isn't that how prisoners were treated?

She came to Charlotte's bedroom door at last. "Fine," she said. "Get a piece of fruit and a glass of water, but if you slip off outside, you will be in the worst trouble you've ever been in, I promise you."

"Mom, if you'd just listen—"

"No, Charlotte," she turned away, not even looking at Charlotte now. "I told you. There's *no* explanation good enough to offer why you and that boy went into a locked church. None. Please do not talk to me about this again!"

CHAPTER
EIGHTEEN

Downstairs, Mr. Abernathy sat at the table, his face troubled, his round eyes fixed on her.

"Tell me what's going on, child," he said the moment she entered the room.

"We went looking for information about you, you know," she said as she sat down across from him.

He nodded. "Your mother wanted to go with you, but she came back alone."

She told him about how they'd explored the cemetery, finding his grave and others, and how they tried to look in the windows. "We were in the church just five or ten minutes, that's all."

"I am appalled!"

She frowned at him. "Well, good grief, Mr. A, we were doing it to help you—"

He held up one pudgy hand. "No, no, my dear. I'm not appalled by *you*, but by the situation. Surely the authorities could see two children such as your-self and E.Z. had set out to cause no harm."

She nodded eagerly. "I know, right? But no one will listen to either one of us. And the more I try to get mom to listen to me, the madder she gets."

He leaned forward and reached out as if to pat her hand. The air stirred cold above it.

"Your mother wants to protect you. She's only doing what she thinks is right."

She slouched in her chair and huffed loudly. "Yeah, well, she's a giant pain. I wish I lived with my dad."

"Charlotte Franklin!" Mom stood in the kitchen doorway. "You were to come down for a snack not to sit here and talk to invisible, imaginary friends. *Get back to your room this instant*!"

Mr. Abernathy's mouth dropped open. "Well, I say. How utterly unnerving you are, madam!"

"She can't hear you, remember," Charlotte said to him. "Even if she could, she wouldn't."

She pushed past Mom and fled upstairs.

She started to slam her door, but then she heard Mom yelling at someone. This time she wasn't talking to Charlotte. Putting one foot quietly in front of the other, she crept back down the steps.

"… and if you are real, you leave my daughter alone, do you hear me?" Mom shouted. "You have no right to disrupt our lives this way. Get out, out, *OUT of my house*!"

"Wow!" Charlotte mouthed silently.

"Upon my honor, woman!" Mr. Abernathy shouted back, though Mom couldn't hear him. "You have no right to speak to me in that manner or to order me out of my own home."

Of course her mom didn't reply to that.

Charlotte hurried to her room before Mom could catch her listening. She leaned against the closed door. Her mother had to be the most unreasonable woman on the face of the earth! She told herself if she ever had kids, she would let them talk, and she'd listen to what they said.

When Dad pulled into the driveway that evening, she burst out of her room to go down to meet him.

"Back to your room, Coco Charlotte Franklin," Mom said from the bottom of the staircase. "You will stay there until I tell you to come out."

Charlotte felt her entire body go stiff. "I want to see my dad!"

Her mother narrowed her eyes. "Not until I talk to him first. Back to your room. Go. *Now*."

Charlotte stayed in her room, pacing and fuming. She could hear the rise and fall of her parents' voices but not what they said. A couple of times, Mr. Abernathy hollered at them, even though they couldn't hear him. His speaking up gave her a warm, fuzzy feeling in her chest, because she knew he cared.

Sometime after dark, there was a soft knock on her door. "Charlotte? It's your daddy, honey."

She flung open the door and threw herself at him.

"I'm so glad to see you, Dad. Mom is completely unreasonable. She won't let me explain anything."

"Shhh," he said softly. "It'll be all right." He sat down on the side of the bed and patted a place next to him. "Tell me what happened."

Charlotte called on the reporter skills she'd been practicing and told her dad exactly what had happened, unemotionally as possible, and in logical order.

"And Dad," she said, lowering her voice, although Mom was downstairs and couldn't hear, "she knows Mr. Abernathy is real. I heard her talking to him today."

"Oh? Well, well." He pondered that for a minute. "I want you to pack a bag, Charlotte. You're coming home with me."

Her heart soared, and she nearly broke her face with a grin. He held up one hand. "Just the rest of this week, until Sunday. You're not moving back to Macomb for good."

Her soaring heart dropped like a rock in a pool. "Why not?"

"Because your mom needs you, sweetheart. She needs you."

How many times had she heard that? Mom would get lost in her head and liable to leave water running in the bathtub for hours. Or forget to turn off the gas. Or lock the doors. That's one reason Great-Grandmum Ellen had visited her, to remind her how much she was needed. But all that talk about being patient and helping Mom stay on her path and all that stuff.... Charlotte didn't even want to think about it. It made her tired inside her head.

"Your mom also needs a few days alone, so we'll give her that," he said. "Go get your things together, and we'll leave in a little while. I have something to take care of, and then I'll be back for you."

After their shopping trip the last time, Charlotte had plenty of clothes at Dad's house. She threw her notebook, some pens, and a couple of books into her backpack, then sat halfway down the steps, waiting. She wanted to go into the kitchen to tell Mr. Abernathy goodbye, but Mom was in there.

When Dad returned about an hour later, Charlotte went downstairs. Mom came out of the kitchen with a small box.

"Here, honey. Boiled oatmeal cookies for you. I know you like them." She kissed Charlotte and gave her an uncertain smile.

Charlotte took the box with the warm cookies inside, realizing this was Mom's way of showing she cared, even if she was still mad.

"Thanks, Mom." Then, although she knew she might get in even worse trouble, she called out, "I'll be back in a few days, Mr. A." She hoped he heard her, because he needed her far more than Mom did.

Mom frowned. "Oh, Charlotte, really. See, David? That's what I mean. She's incorrigible."

"Let it go, Jen. Come on, Charlotte." He took her bag and opened the door. "We'll be back Sunday. 'Bye, Jen."

Charlotte forced out her next words. "'Bye, Mom. Thanks for the cookies." She wanted to say, "I love you," but somehow she was too upset to get the words out.

"Dad, it was not what it seemed," she said as they walked to the car. "We weren't trying to cause a problem, and we didn't swipe anything, or break anything—"

He opened the passenger door. "Get in, hon. We'll discuss this later."

She sighed loudly and wondered why no one would let her talk. Poor Mr. Abernathy must feel a hundred times worse than she did. A thousand times worse. No one but she could hear him.

She got in and closed the door.

"Hey, Charlotte."

She jumped with surprise and whirled to look in the backseat. "E.Z.! Why are you here? My dad will—"

Her dad got in the car and fastened his seatbelt. He grinned at them both. "E.Z. is spending the rest of the week with us too."

Charlotte could hardly believe her eyes and ears. "For real?"

"For real."

"What did Mom say?"

He backed out of the driveway and asked, "Wham Burger for dinner?"

"Awesome!" E.Z. said, grinning.

"Yes, but what did Mom say about E.Z. coming too?"

"I'll explain to your mother another time."

Which meant he'd said nothing at all to her. Wow.

"But, Dad—"

"We've got the rest of the week, Charlotte. Let's enjoy it."

"But what about your work?"

He turned his head and grinned at her. "I wangled some time off. You two are stuck with me until Sunday."

When they got to the house, her dad showed E.Z. the guest room he'd be staying in.

"Dude. A real bed with pillows and everything. Does that TV work? Wow, a TV in my room." He opened a door on the other side and peeked in. "My own bathroom!"

Charlotte and her dad grinned at each other and shared a silent fist bump. E.Z. talked so much that night, Charlotte was sure he would lose his voice.

❦

While her friend was showering the next morning, Charlotte talked with Dad.

"I'm real glad E.Z. is here with us, but how did you, er, I mean, does his mother know…I mean…."

"You mean how did I get him here?"

She nodded.

"I went over to his house to talk with his grandmother. But I took one step into that place, saw how the kid lives, and flashed my badge. I told her he was coming with me."

Her eyes got big. "No way! What did she say?"

He grimaced. "She said 'Good riddance!'"

"Wow. What about his mother?"

"Before I came and got you, I drove down to Tim's Grill. She said, 'Fine. Keep him as long as you want him. He's worthless.'"

She stared at him, swallowing hard as tears filled her eyes and spilled over. She didn't even try to stop them. "Oh, Daddy! How can anyone be so mean?"

"I don't know, baby girl. It's not fair, is it?"

She shook her head and hugged him hard. She was glad he was her father, but she surely wished E.Z. had someone as good as her dad in his life. Even as scattered and thoughtless as she could be, Charlotte knew Mom loved her. She would never carelessly let her go off with a stranger in the night.

Her dad fired up the grill and cooked their breakfast outside. He even baked biscuits in a covered iron skillet. Charlotte was sure no breakfast had ever been so tasty. E. Z. ate so much, Charlotte thought his stomach might burst.

When the last biscuit was eaten, Dad sat back in his chair. He folded his arms and studied them both. She recognized that serious expression. This is how he looked whenever she got in trouble. Even though she'd been expecting this conversation and the scolding that was sure to follow, Charlotte's heart sank.

"So now that you've had a good night's sleep and been well-fed, and you're comfortable," he said, "I want the two of you to tell me why you thought it was such a bright idea to break into a church."

Charlotte shot a glance at E.Z., who looked like he'd been kicked in the stomach by a mule.

"We didn't mean to," she said.

Her dad narrowed his eyes and never blinked. His lashes didn't even flutter. "No one ever accidently breaks into a place."

"It was my fault," E.Z. said. "Charlotte has nothing to do with it. If you want to send me back home, or put me in jail, or whatever, go ahead. But Charlotte had nothing to do with it."

Her dad shifted his gaze ever so slightly to bore into E.Z.'s anxious eyes.

"The fact is, you went into a locked building, and you were caught by the police. Charlotte was with you. Now. Tell me why."

Charlotte spoke up.

"Because of Mr. Abernathy. I told you about him, Dad. I told you I wanted to find out who killed him, and he said he thought the records would be in a book in that church, and we thought maybe we could find a clue or something in it."

His hard gaze did not flicker. She went on.

"I asked you about investigating this, you know. I took notes. We have names and questions to ask people."

"And where in that conversation did I suggest you break into a locked building?"

She swallowed hard and almost wished she had

stayed in Park City.

"It was my fault, Mr. Franklin. I swear it." E.Z. raised one hand as if he were taking an oath in court.

"No!" Charlotte said. "E.Z., stop trying to take all the blame for this. I could've told you any time 'Let's leave.' Instead, I wanted to find out so we could help Mr. A."

"But, Charlotte—" he began, but she interrupted him.

"So, Dad?"

"So, Charlotte?"

"What are you going to do to us?" she asked him.

He fixed his stony gaze on E.Z. "Where did you learn to pick a lock?"

"One of Ma's boyfriends showed me how."

"And this was okay with your mother?"

E.Z.'s face reddened. "She don't care."

"I'm sure she doesn't want you breaking the law and getting a criminal record."

E.Z. looked down and refused to lift his head or reply.

Dad shifted his eyes to Charlotte. "Have you two done things like this before?"

"No!"

E.Z. jerked his head up. "No way, Mr. Franklin. We just wanted to help Mr. A."

"That's all, Daddy. Honest. We didn't take anything or break anything, or mess with anything at all. We were just looking for that book."

"Did you think to call the pastor of that church, or maybe send him a text, asking if you could look at the book?"

"No, sir," they said in unison, subdued.

"Did you ask anyone for any help, at any time?"

"Just that cranky old woman at the library. And Shoji. But I told you about them, Dad. Remember?"

"So that list of questions you said you wrote…." He raised one eyebrow questioningly.

"I never got a chance to ask anyone. E.Z. and I had a plan, but before we could do anything, Mom said we couldn't ever spend time together again, and she locked me in my room to make sure."

"Now, Charlotte, I know your mother *did not* lock you in your room."

She huffed. "Well, not with a lock and key, but she wouldn't let me step outside of it, so I might as well have been in jail."

E.Z. leaned forward, all the sadness gone from his face, and his eyes had an eager light in them. "When you say questions, you mean those ones we talked about? The ones in your notebook?"

Charlotte nodded.

He grinned and jumped up from his chair. He paced around a bit and said "Dude!" at least five times.

"Sit down, son, and tell us what's got you excited." Her dad was calm and polite, but firm.

"After Mrs. F. threw me out of the house and locked Charlotte in her room—"

Dad frowned. "She didn't lock Charlotte in her room."

"Okay. But anyway, I knew Granny wouldn't want me in the house, bothering her while she watched Jerry Springer, so I went to the Golden Sunset Manor. That nursing home on the edge of town, near the hospital."

A shiver went all through Charlotte. "What happened?"

"I went inside and there was a big living room with all these old folks sitting around watching the television, so I started asking them about all those people on that list, trying to find out if any of them were related, or maybe knew someone who was."

His grin nearly split his face. Charlotte thought she might burst into a thousand shivering pieces of anticipation.

"What?" she screamed. "E.Z., what happened?"

"There's this old lady, Peggy Sue Martin, living there who is the niece of Minerva Van Elder."

"The housekeeper!" Charlotte gasped. She leaned forward, her eyes wide. "Did you see her, did you talk to her? Did you ask her any of those questions? What did she say?"

"Charlotte," her dad said, putting one hand on her arm. "Let the boy talk."

"Okay, okay! Talk, E.Z." She curled her hands into balls to keep them from shaking with her excitement.

"So this old dude says, 'Come with me, boy. I'll innerduce y'uns.' So we're walking down the hall and all those old folks are in the rooms, and they're sleeping or just staring at the wall." His grin slipped away. "It was really sad how they just sat there, like they'd been told not to move." He glanced away. "Ma, she keeps threatening to send Granny to Golden Sunset, but Granny'd go crazy there. I know she would." He turned back to them. "Anyways, me and this old dude, we're walking down a long hall and this nurse or somebody comes running at us, and grabs my arm and asks me if I'm related to someone there. Then she says if I'm not family, I have to leave."

"No fair!" Charlotte hollered.

"Did you leave?" her dad asked.

"Yeah, man. Charlotte and I had been kicked out of two places already, so I figured I'd get in big trouble if I made a fuss."

The frown on her dad's face made Charlotte wish E.Z. had left some things unsaid. "Kicked out of two places?"

"We went to the Clairmonte," she said before E.Z. could reply. "We thought we might find something or someone there since Mr. A had once been part owner, but it was just a grody old hotel and we left."

"You were kicked out?"

"Asked to leave is all, Dad. The old man behind the desk—"

"His name was Elmo," E.Z. said.

She nodded. "Elmo said it was no place for kids and that the basement had been flooded so no paperwork from long ago was still around. We left. We weren't kicked out. Exactly. Not like we were at the church. No police or anyone like that was there."

Her father shifted his glance from one to the other about four times. "Charlotte, I'm all for you becoming an investigative reporter, if that's what you want to do, but you can't just go barging into certain places. Not at your age, and not without some experience. E.Z., you did the right thing by leaving when you were asked."

He took out a pen and small spiral-topped notebook from his shirt pocket and began writing. Charlotte had never seen her dad without that notebook and pen. She figured some detectives used a smart phone for taking notes, but he never had. It was like he preferred pen and paper. His frown stayed in place as he filled up a couple of pages. When he closed the notebook and returned it to his pocket, his expression relaxed.

"Now," he said, smiling at them both, "how about a trip to the swimming hole? E.Z. did you bring your trunks?"

Her dad had something in mind, but she knew better than to press him about it. He'd let them know when the time was right.

CHAPTER NINETEEN

Sunday afternoon, her dad drove to the Rock Church instead of taking Charlotte and E.Z. home. The two of them exchanged mystified looks but said nothing.

A smiling young man in a clerical collar met them at the front doors. He introduced himself as Reverend Edward Carver and shook everyone's hand.

"I'm David Franklin. I called a couple of days ago about looking at your records book," Dad said.

"Yes, of course. Come inside and have a seat." Reverend Carver led them into the sanctuary and indicated the back pew. He smiled into Charlotte's eyes. "I believe you are the young lady wanting to take a look at those records?"

Did he know the police had hauled her and E.Z. out of the church like criminals? Probably so, but he said nothing about it. Her face grew hot, and she looked at the floor, away from the kind, smiling eyes of the man.

"Yes, sir."

The minister handed her a heavy book with a dark red leather cover. "This is what you want."

"Yes, sir," she whispered.

If E.Z. was as embarrassed as Charlotte, he hid it well. "Whoa! Is that the book with names in it?"

"It is."

"Awesome." He grinned at Charlotte. "See if Mr. A is listed in there."

Charlotte took a deep breath and lifted her gaze. "Thank you, sir. We didn't mean to cause any trouble. We didn't hurt anything, or touch anything. Well, I *did* look in the desk for the book when we didn't find it on the shelf, but I didn't mess with anything inside. And E.Z. played the piano. But that's it."

"I understand." Reverend Carver turned his smile to the boy. "Do you play?"

E.Z. shrugged and flushed to the roots of his hair. Charlotte was amazed breaking into the church and getting caught didn't embarrass him but playing the piano did.

"So, sweetheart, are you going to look for his name?" Her dad dipped his head toward the book she held.

"Yes, sir."

With great care, she turned the pages. E.Z. eagerly leaned in, as if he could read the names.

"There's the date!" he said, pushing the tip of his index finger on the year written out in fancy script— 1929.

By then Charlotte was so excited she forced herself to turn the brittle pages carefully.

"Here's his name," she breathed. "Clarence Albert Abernathy, born March 8, 1878, died of an injury, May 27, 1929."

"What else does it say?"

"Nothing else." She felt like someone had poured cold water on her head. "No new information at all."

"No way!" E.Z. yelped.

After everything they'd done to find this book, and here it was, in her hands, but not a bit of new information in it, not one thing she could use to help Mr. Abernathy. She wanted to either burst into tears or kick something.

"Don't you have anything, *anything* at all about him, Reverend Carver?"

She angrily brushed away a tear that dared to slip free of her lashes.

"I'm sorry, no. But you should talk to Mrs. Shreve at the library. I understand she has a treasure trove of documents."

Charlotte sighed and gazed wistfully at the records book. If she could have one wish right then, it would be to find out what happened to Mr. Abernathy without running into so many dead ends.

She handed the records book back to Reverend Carver. "I tried talking to her, but she acted like nothing was any of my business. I think she knows something, but she refused to tell me."

The doors to the church opened and a tall, thin man

in a sweater and fedora hat came inside.

"Who knows what about who?" He joined the group as if he'd been invited. He didn't even say hello. "Who knows something they won't tell?"

Reverend Carver smiled at the man. "Robert Johnston, why are you here instead of home watching the Cardinals game on television?"

"I saw the two cars parked outside and wondered why someone was at the church on a Sunday afternoon." He passed his nosy glance around to everyone in the group. "So, what's going on?"

"Mr. Johnston is our church secretary," the minister explained. He introduced Charlotte, E.Z., and her dad.

Mr. Johnston gave her father a curt nod and ignored the children. "So, who knows something they aren't telling?"

The man had the beady eyes and primly pursed mouth of a town busybody. Nosy people always knew a lot of stuff. Hope swelled in Charlotte's heart.

"I asked Mrs. Shreve at the library if she knew anything about C.A. Abernathy," she told him, "and she said she didn't, but I think she did. She acted like she did."

The man squinted his pale brown eyes at her. "C.A. Abernathy who helped to found the bank?"

"Yes! Do you know anything about him?"

"Not him, I don't, except he helped to start the Bank of Park City, and later on he and his partner, Horatio Lawson, ran the hotel. He built that big fine house over on Timberline, when it was a nice street. It's all gone to pot now. Not to be outdone by Abernathy and his house, Lawson built one almost like it—only bigger and fancier—over on Five Acre, but they bulldozed most of that street to build the Walmart back in '92. Shame the way the town has spread out north of town. All the old houses have been left to rack and ruin."

Mr. Johnston took the conversation in a direction that Charlotte cared nothing about.

"Well, I'm pretty sure Mrs. Shreve knows more about Mr. Abernathy than she's letting on," Charlotte said. "But you might know more than she does."

Mr. Johnston seemed to swell in importance. Just as Charlotte hoped, he offered more information. "Lawson was Mrs. Shreve's great-grandfather. And there was some funny business going on in this town because of him, but it ended when he died in 1929. That funny business is why Mrs. Shreve doesn't want to talk to you." He tapped the side of his nose and winked. "She's a proud woman and doesn't want any gossip going on about her ancestors. She's done well to cover up most of it, but you can't hide everything from everyone."

"What funny business?" E.Z. asked.

"That's not my place to say."

"Don't you know?" Charlotte prodded.

He looked uncomfortable, as if she'd just poked a pin in his self-importance balloon. "It's been a well-kept secret all this time."

"Then I have to go back and talk to her again."

"Yeah. We gotta!" E.Z. got to his feet as if he'd take off running to the library right then.

"Hold it. Sit down." Charlotte's dad reached out and gently tugged E.Z.'s arm until the boy sat down.

"I don't think the library is open on Sunday, anyway," Charlotte said.

"That woman won't tell you a blessed thing unless she wants to," Mr. Johnston said. "And I can guarantee she doesn't want to. Nor will she."

Charlotte figured if Mrs. Shreve kept her family history a secret, it was likely her great-grandfather or one of his family killed Mr. Abernathy so the Lawsons would have full ownership of the hotel. She and E.Z. exchanged glances as if they were thinking the same thing.

"Now, I'll tell you what you can do," Mr. Johnston said, his bumptiousness returning. "You might find someone over at the Golden Sunset Manor who might know something about the old guy." Mr. Johnston squinted at her as if trying to read her mind. "But see here. Why are you so all-fired interested in this C.A. Abernathy? He never was some big movie star or athlete or singer. He was just a banker in a small town. Why should you care anything about him?"

Mr. Johnston might be a good one to get gossip and tales from, but he seemed far too interested in something that was none of his business. If she told him about her gift and why she needed the information about Mr. Abernathy, tomorrow morning her face might be on the front page of the *Park City Courier*, under the headlines,

"New Girl in Town Sees Dead People."

E.Z., however, didn't have any compunction about sharing plans with this Nosy Norman. "We're gonna go talk to Peggy Sue Martin, over at Golden Sunset Manor."

Mr. Johnston snapped his fingers and pointed at E.Z. "That's right! She's a relative of his housekeeper. Worked for old Doc Witter, the vet. Never did marry."

"Sir," Charlotte said, "you seem to know an awful lot about Park City history. Why is Mrs. Shreve the town historian instead of you?"

"Because, young miss, I'm not part of the old families." He pushed out his chest and lifted his nose. "But I know far more than Harriet Shreve or any of the other townsfolks realize."

"Maybe you and Mrs. Shreve could share the job," she suggested.

He snorted. "That woman will not give an inch, not the merest inch."

"Too bad." Charlotte twisted her mouth.

"But you still haven't told me why you are so interested in C.A. Abernathy." He shifted his snooping expression to Charlotte's dad.

Instead of explaining the situation to him, Dad stood up. "We've taken up enough of your Sunday afternoon, Pastor. And yours, too, Mr. Johnston. Thank you for your help."

Mr. Johnston looked deflated again. Charlotte hoped he wouldn't follow them to the nursing home, poking his long nose into their business.

Her dad shook hands with both men. Charlotte and

E.Z. followed his example, just like grown people, courteous and friendly, but still serious. She thanked them both. It was important business, helping Mr. Abernathy.

CHAPTER TWENTY

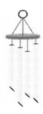

Golden Sunset Manor looked like a cross between a motel and hospital. Instead of a grassy lawn, there was a big parking lot, and no trees anywhere. Just the hard look of the place made Charlotte feel depressed.

Inside, it practically glowed with cleanliness. The strong odor of bleach pinched her nostrils. The big room right across from the receptionist's desk had a large television. Several white-haired people sat watching the news channel. A few of them turned to look at Charlotte, her dad, and E.Z. She smiled at them while her dad talked to the woman at the desk.

"Come on, kids," he said after their brief conversation. "Let's go see Miss Martin."

"You mean they're going to let me go, too?" E.Z. asked, hanging back a little.

"Sure. Come on."

They found Peggy Sue Martin in room 198. She sat

near the window in a small rocking chair, her white head bent as she knitted something pink.

Charlotte's father knocked on her open door, and she looked up.

"Hello?" Her gaze took in the trio then stayed on him.

"Miss Martin?" he said.

She nodded her head once.

Charlotte stepped forward. "Hi. I'm Charlotte Franklin. This is my dad, David, and my friend E.Z. Bishop."

The woman took off her glasses and ran her gaze over each one again.

"I don't believe I know any of you," she said.

"No, ma'am. But would you be willing to talk to us for a little while?"

Miss Martin folded her hands on top of her glasses and her knitting. "What is it you want to talk about?"

Charlotte cleared her throat so her words would be distinct, in case Miss Martin had trouble hearing.

"I'm, er, I mean, *we* are trying to find information about Clarence Albert Abernathy. Someone said you're related to Minerva Van Elder, his housekeeper."

The old woman's mouth opened and shut a couple of times as if she didn't know what to say. "My goodness. Aunt Minerva. I haven't thought of her in years."

"You remember her?" E.Z. asked.

"I do. A fearful old woman who kept to herself." She looked at Charlotte's dad. "Why are you asking about

Aunt Minerva?"

Charlotte thought maybe it was best to let her father talk right then.

"Actually, my daughter and wife have recently moved into the Abernathy house on Timberline Avenue, and Charlotte has become interested in the history of the place. In the little bit of history she's found, she's uncovered what seems to be the mysterious death of Mr. Abernathy. We're hoping you can help shed some light on what actually happened."

Miss Martin seemed to shrink back a little in her chair. "Oh. That."

Charlotte bit her lip. "What do you mean?"

The woman waved one thin hand as if waving away something bothersome.

"It all happened so long ago...I don't see what possible good it is for you to know the details."

Charlotte's father sat on the edge of the bed and leaned forward, resting his elbows on his knees. He looked earnestly and kindly at her. He was being Charlotte's gentle, good dad, but he was also being dad-the-detective.

"Ma'am, it's not our intent to upset you, or cause you any pain. Is it, kids?" He looked over his shoulder at them and beckoned them to draw near. "But a murder case is never closed until it is solved. And we'd surely like to solve this one. Put the memory and name of Clarence Abernathy to rest."

"Murder? You think he was murdered?"

Charlotte's dad sat back. She and E.Z. looked at each other. Mr. Abernathy had believed so firmly that someone had killed him, Charlotte never seriously considered anything else.

"You don't believe he was murdered?"

Silence fell. It lingered so long that Charlotte wondered if the woman would ever speak to them again.

"Not … exactly." She looked uncomfortable.

"How's that?" Charlotte's dad tipped one ear toward her.

"He wasn't exactly murdered. It was sort of an accident."

"Sort of?" E.Z. echoed.

She straightened her back. "Mr. Franklin, I'm not sure I ought to divulge this. After all, Aunt Minerva never meant for it to happen, and she surely never meant for the details to get spread around."

"I understand. But, ma'am, it's been a long time, nearly a hundred years." He paused to let this sink in. "Don't you think it's time for the truth to come out?"

Another long silence.

"Ma'am?" Dad said, very quietly. "No one can be hurt any more. If anyone was guilty of anything, they have long passed away and the deed with them."

"That's right." She nodded vigorously. "So why can't we just let it lie?"

"Because, ma'am, keeping the truth buried isn't right, on any level. In her research, my daughter has built an 'affection,' if you will, for Mr. Abernathy. She's interested in his life, in his accomplishments, and in his death. What if Mr. Abernathy's spirit is uneasy because of the secretive nature of his death? Doesn't he deserve to rest in peace? If not for the memory of the deceased, won't you at least give Charlotte the satisfaction of knowing what happened to this man?"

Miss Martin frowned and fidgeted. She huffed out a long breath and fiddled with the pink yarn in her lap.

"Oh, all right. I suppose it can't hurt. Not after all this time."

Now they were getting somewhere, at last. It was all Charlotte could do to sit still and act mature.

Miss Martin turned her eyes to Charlotte. "That man your daddy says you've built an affection for wasn't very popular. In fact, according to my aunt, he was fussy, critical, and lacking in gratitude."

Charlotte knew exactly what Miss Martin's aunt had meant. Mr. Abernathy, the ghost, was persnickety and expected others to be just as exacting. She was sure he'd been the same way when he was alive. But maybe Minerva Van Elder had never really talked to Mr. Abernathy. Maybe all she had done was clean his house and cook, but never tried to get to know him.

She spoke her thoughts aloud. "Maybe he was just lonely and didn't know how to get along with others."

Miss Martin raised her index finger. "Or maybe he was lonely because he was so unlikable."

"Or unlikable because he was lonely."

Miss Martin blinked at her as if she'd never thought

of it that way. "Nevertheless, Aunt Minerva worked hard for him for twenty years, six days a week, and he never gave her a word of thanks or a raise in salary. She deserved some respect and gratitude."

"Yes, ma'am. So what happened? Why did he die?"

She plucked at the yarn for a few seconds. "He liked his floors clean and shining. Every day she had to mop every room in that big house, whether or not someone had been in those rooms." She passed around a look to make sure they were all listening. "Aunt Minerva was supposed to do her work while he was at the bank, but she decided she'd take the day off on her birthday. For once in her life, she wanted to celebrate it by not working. She made his breakfast and had fixed his evening meal. It was in the ice box already. Her intention was to leave as soon as he went to work. To her mind, she kept that house so clean, the old man would never know she'd skipped a day."

She hesitated, and for a moment Charlotte was afraid she wasn't going to finish, but she drew in a deep breath and blew it out.

"She had spilled some grease on the floor when she made his breakfast that morning, and in her excitement to get away, she didn't notice. When he came downstairs, he stepped in the grease. His feet slid out from under him, and he fell backward. His head hit the corner of the stove, then slammed against that hard floor. His skull popped like a dropped egg."

"Poor Mr. Abernathy!" Charlotte gasped.

Miss Martin nodded. "Aunt Minerva had gone outside to get the newspaper, and when she came back, there he was, dead, blood spreading out...." She shuddered.

"I see." Charlotte's dad's voice was very quiet.

"It was an accident," E.Z. said.

"A tragic accident," her dad said, nodding. "But, ma'am, why did your aunt want to keep it a secret?"

She reached out and grabbed his hand. "Don't you see? If she'd done her job right, the way she was supposed to, it wouldn't have happened. If she'd washed the grease off the floor when she spilled it ... ." She chewed her lower lip for a moment, as though pondering whether to continue. She drew in a deep breath and blew it out as she let go of his hand. "After it happened, she was afraid the police would arrest her, so she scrubbed the floor around and under him and even wiped off his shoes. She dried everything so no one would know she'd cleaned up the grease that caused him to fall. Then she called the police."

"That's rotten!" E.Z. said.

Charlotte gouged him with her elbow.

Her dad laid his hand gently on Miss Martin's arm, just for a moment. "Thank you, ma'am, for telling us. Although what your aunt did wasn't ethical, it wasn't a crime. If she lived out her life in guilt and fear, she punished herself far more than the simple reprimand she would have received from the police."

"She didn't tell anyone else?" Charlotte asked.

Miss Martin shook her head. "She only shared her story with the family, and none of us ever spoke a word to anyone."

"The police never investigated this death?" Dad asked.

"I don't think so. I believe it was fairly cut and dried, an accident. If there had been any suspicions that Mr. Abernathy had been murdered, I'm pretty sure they would have looked at Horatio Lawson, Jr."

"Why?" E.Z. asked, leaning forward eagerly.

"Because that man was as crooked as the day is long. And jealous. He wanted everything Abernathy had. He swindled the man out of his share of the hotel and embezzled money from the bank. But that didn't come to light until after Horatio died."

"Wow," Charlotte said. "No wonder Mrs. Shreve wouldn't tell me anything."

"Harriet Shreve?" Miss Martin said with a derisive chuckle. "No, she wouldn't. Not that one. She's mighty proud of being one of Park City's oldest and wealthiest families, and she'd never air their dirty laundry."

"I wonder if Mr. A had any idea his partner was a swindler," E.Z. said.

"That's something I couldn't tell you," the old woman said.

"I bet he didn't know," Charlotte piped up. "If he'd known that, he wouldn't have gone into business with him. Mr. A is a lot smarter than that."

Miss Martin gave her a curious stare.

"I mean, I bet he was a lot smarter than that, being one of the founders of the bank and all."

"I'm sure you're right," her dad said quickly. He got to his feet. "In any case, you have helped us a great deal, Miss Martin, and we appreciate it."

Miss Martin held onto him after they'd shaken hands. "You won't mention to Harriet Shreve that I told you anything, will you?" She looked concerned but held his gaze steady with her own.

"I won't say a word, and neither will the kids." He looked at them. "Right?"

"Right," they replied in unison.

CHAPTER TWENTY-ONE

Charlotte's dad dropped E.Z. off in front of the little white house, then parked in the driveway where she and Mom lived.

"I want to talk privately with your mom. While I'm doing that, you can tell Mr. Abernathy the news without the worry of being interrupted."

"You're going to talk to Mom?" She hoped, hoped, *hoped* he was going to talk to her about their getting back together.

"I am."

She grinned, jumped out of the car, and ran into the house.

"Mom, I'm home!" she yelled as she dashed up the stairs. "And Dad wants to talk to you."

"Charlotte?" Mom came out of the kitchen and stood at the foot of the stairs, looking up at her. "I'm making your favorite sloppy-joes for dinner."

She ran back down and gave Mom a hug. "It smells awesome."

Dad came inside and offered his wife a smile. "Hi, Jen. You look nice."

Her hair was combed, and she was wearing a green and white checked sundress and green sandals. She even had a bit of lipstick on. Had she fixed supper and dressed up pretty because he would be there?

"Dad wants to talk to you, don't you, Dad?"

She grabbed his hand, tugged him forward, then pushed him toward Mom. "Why don't you two go upstairs and have a nice chat in private." She peeked into the kitchen, saw that Mom hadn't finished cooking. At the table, Mr. Abernathy looked at her hopefully. "I'll make sure the sloppy joes don't burn."

Mom frowned. "Charlotte, I don't—"

"Come on, Jen." Dad took her hand. "Show me what you're working on in your studio."

The woman blinked as if completely surprised. "Really?"

"Of course really. I realize I haven't given you the support I should've all this time. So show me what you're doing."

"Well, if you want to see it …."

"I do."

Charlotte stood at the foot of the steps, smiling, watching them as they went upstairs. She made a wish and crossed her fingers, hard. Then, with a happy sigh, she practically skipped into the kitchen.

"Welcome home, child. It's so nice to have you back." Mr. Abernathy smiled from ear to ear. "I hope you had a good time with your father."

She sat down across from him. Her heart warmed, knowing he'd missed her.

"I did! And guess what? E.Z. went to Dad's too."

His eyebrows went up.

"But your mother forbade you to spend time with that young man. I heard her."

"She did. It was Dad's idea to take E.Z. with us. Mom doesn't know. It was great. I don't think E.Z. has ever spent time with a man like my dad." She grinned. "Guess what, Mr. A?"

"My dear," he intoned as he adjusted the cuffs of his shirt, "as you grow to know me better, you'll realize I dislike guessing games."

"I have news for you!"

She thought he would have stood and shouted with delight. Instead, he stared at her with his round eyes growing bigger.

"Pray tell me, child. Why are you making a game of this? I should not have to beg for news."

For a ghost, he could be so exasperating sometimes. "I wasn't trying to make a game or cause you to beg. I was simply making the most of the suspense, like opening a Christmas present."

He sniffed and smoothed his jacket, as if her words had wrinkled it. "Yes, well. Pray continue."

"We—that is, Dad, E.Z., and I—found out what

happened to you."

"Eh? How's that?" He got up, walked around the table once and sat back down "Wha ... you ... you ... f-f-found out ...? Who? Who was the rotten scoundrel that killed me?"

"No one."

He scowled so hard, his frown nearly reached the back of his skull.

"Don't be foolish, child. I'm dead, aren't I?"

"But you weren't murdered, Mr. A."

He shimmered and faded until she could see through him, then his usual appearance returned, but he looked paler than before.

"Not...murdered?"

"No, sir."

His entire face drooped, along with his shoulders. His disappointment completely dumbfounded Charlotte. She tipped her head to one side and studied him.

"Isn't this good news, Mr. A? All this time, you've believed someone hated you enough to murder you, but no one did. Isn't that good news to you?"

He sputtered a moment then burst out with, "Of course I was murdered. I felt a hard blow to the back of my head. I saw my body lying there, with blood pooling around me, and the police carrying me out. I stood right next to that stove and saw my dead body. I was killed, I tell you. *Killed*!"

He was so agitated he paled and almost disappeared again.

"Yes, Mr. A, you were killed, but—"

"Aha! I knew it!"

"But you weren't *murdered*. You stepped in some grease Minerva had spilled on the floor, and your feet went out from under you. You smacked your head on the corner of the stove then on this hard floor. It was an *accident*, not murder."

He gawped at her. The shimmering waves that passed through him slowed as he digested the information.

"How, er, um," He cleared his throat. "How do you know this information?"

"We found Minerva's niece today. Minerva had told her family, but no one else. You see, she'd neglected to clean the spill, and she felt terribly guilty about it. For the rest of her life, she blamed herself for your death."

"But Minerva was a wonderful housekeeper. Leaving grease on the floor was unlike anything she'd do."

Charlotte nodded. "Right. That's one reason she felt so guilty. Because she hadn't cleaned the floor properly."

He fiddled with his bow tie and lapels. "Dear, dear, dear," he muttered. "Mercy, mercy, mercy."

While Mr. Abernathy fidgeted and muttered, Charlotte got up and stirred the simmering sloppy joes. Not for the first time did she think how strange it was that the original kitchen stove still worked and how she could cook food where Minerva Van Elder had prepared Mr. Abernathy's meals.

"Say!" he said suddenly.

"What's up, Mr. A?" she said, sitting down again.

"You said 'That's one reason she felt so guilty.' Was there more than one reason?"

She hesitated, unsure if he was ready for more news. "Promise you won't get upset and shimmery?"

"Whatever does that mean? Getting 'shimmery,' indeed."

"I mean, don't get so worked up that you nearly disappear. It's downright spooky when you do that."

He frowned. "I do not shimmer."

"You shimmer right before you disappear. You shimmer like a soap bubble."

He waggled his mouth open and shut a few times. "If I do, I assure you it is unintentional."

"Just don't get upset."

"Child, you are stretching my patience."

She sought for the right words to share with him. "Minerva felt as if you didn't fully appreciate her work," she said slowly, in a very low voice.

He jerked as if someone had poked him. "I say! What's that?"

"She told the family you never expressed gratitude or gave her a raise in salary."

He jerked on his lapels and jacket sleeves so hard, Charlotte was afraid he'd rip the fabric—if ghost fabric could rip.

"Perhaps she never understood my gratitude."

"Did you ever say, 'Thank you'?"

He refused to meet her eyes. "I don't remember details."

"Did you ever give her a raise in pay?"

"What does that have to do with anything? I paid her more generously than anyone else in this town would have done. And I gave her a generous bonus every year at Christmas."

"Miss Martin never mentioned that. Maybe Minerva never told her family about bonuses."

"Hmphf! And you call me ungrateful. Tsk, tsk, tsk."

"I didn't call you anything, Mr. A. I just told you what I found out. And if I were you, I'd be glad that no one hated me enough to murder me."

He sighed, long and deep. A chill stirred the air. "You do have a point."

"And now, maybe you can move on, out of this kitchen and into whatever lies before you in the next world."

To Charlotte's surprise, sadness filled his expression. A different kind of sadness than she'd seen on his face before.

"Mr. A? What's wrong?"

He looked down and twisted a button on his vest as if he'd never seen it before. "Well, my dear, the fact is…truth to tell…." He lifted his gaze. "I'll miss you when I'm gone. I never thought I'd ever be friends with a little girl, er, a young girl. Or any child, for that matter. But since you've been here, why, my stay has been pleasant. Quite pleasant."

She wasn't sure if ghosts could cry, but she thought she saw tears in his eyes.

"That's so sweet, Mr. Abernathy."

"Sweet?" He looked appalled.

"Nice, then, if you prefer."

He nodded his head once. "And I meant every word."

"The thing is, Dad is upstairs talking to Mom, and I think he's going to talk her into going back home. Back to Macomb."

Mr. Abernathy's entire round face once more drooped like a deflated balloon.

"But if you move on, away from this kitchen," she said, "then you won't miss me, because you'll be...well, wherever spirits go when it's time to leave the earth."

The door of Mom's studio opened, and her parents came downstairs, talking softly to each other. They entered the kitchen, but Charlotte couldn't tell if they'd made up or not.

"Charlotte," Mom said, "would you please run across the street and ask E.Z. to come over?"

"For real?"

Her mom nodded.

"Go get him, Charlotte." Her dad smiled and gave her a big wink.

Knowing Mom wanted to talk to E.Z. made her very happy. The possibility of returning to Macomb as a family filled her with hope. And yet she wanted to help Mr. Abernathy cross over if she could. What if he left on his own while she was out of the kitchen? She looked at him.

He smiled at her. "Go on, child. Go get your friend."

CHAPTER TWENTY-TWO

E.Z. was sitting on the steps of his sagging front porch. He carefully oiled the back wheels of his skateboard with a small blue can of WD-40. He looked up when Charlotte dashed across the street.

"Hey!"

"Hey! Mom wants you to come over."

"Huh?" He nearly dropped the skateboard.

"C'mon. Mom and Dad want you to come over to the house."

"Me?"

She put both hands on her hips and gave him a sour look. "Who else is out here but you and me?"

"But I thought—"

She grabbed his hand and tugged. "Put your board down and come with me. Before she changes her mind."

He laid the skateboard on the porch next to the WD-40, and they sprinted to the yellow house.

"Whoa!" E.Z. said the minute they stepped through the front door. "It smells awesome in here."

"That's Mom's famous sloppy joes. She makes them better than anyone."

They went into the kitchen and Charlotte stopped in surprise to see the table set for four people. Her dad was emptying a bag of chips into a bowl, and Mom was scooping the fragrant spicy meat onto buns.

E.Z.'s grin spread all over his face. Then, "I'll be right back."

Before anyone could stop him, he darted out of the kitchen and out of the house.

"I bet he's bringing some SpaghettiOs or something," Charlotte said.

She was almost right. He came back with four cans of Pepsi-Cola. She helped him to wipe the moisture off the ice-cold cans and put one at each place setting.

Mr. Abernathy stood away from the table, next to the back door, as if he would open it and walk out at any moment. He smiled at Charlotte but said nothing as everyone settled down to eat.

"Before we eat," Mom said, touching her gold necklace, "I have something to say."

They looked at her expectantly. She gave E.Z. a nervous smile. "E.Z., my husband told me you spent these last few days in Macomb with him and Charlotte."

His face grew red, and he ducked his head for moment, as if he'd done something wrong. But then he straightened and met her eyes. "Yes, ma'am. I was invited."

"I know." She smiled at him. "I also know about your circumstances at home."

He nodded, still looking uncomfortable.

"And I understand why you and my daughter broke into a church."

"Mom, that wasn't E.Z.'s—"

"Charlotte, I'm talking to E.Z. right now. Now, E.Z., while I can never condone breaking and entering, Mr. Franklin has explained everything. He believes this will never happen again. Yes?"

He gulped. "Yes, ma'am."

"And you understand if it does, there will be no more second chances for the two of you to spend time together."

"Yes, ma'am."

She transferred her stern gaze to her daughter.

"I understand, Mom. It won't happen again."

Mom shifted her gaze back and forth between them a few times. Satisfied at last, she gave them each a smile.

"Good. As long as you remember that rule, the two of you may spend time together."

Charlotte and E.Z. grinned at each other.

"Now," Mom said, picking up the platter of warm sandwiches, "who wants a sloppy joe?"

Later, after Dad went home and Mom washed the dinner dishes, Charlotte and E.Z. sat outside on the steps of the front porch and watched the lightning bugs. The sound of tree frogs and crickets made a pleasant music in the warm air.

Neither parent mentioned getting back together, or a return soon to Macomb. It was a disappointment, but right then, Charlotte was content to know that they were talking to each other and getting along. Plus, as much as she missed Macomb, her home there, and her dad, she was happy to spend time with E.Z. He was a good friend who never made fun of her or ridiculed Mom like Chloe or Olivia used to. Plus, he was dependable. Charlotte now realized she preferred spending time with someone she could rely on.

"I think it's so cool that you can play the piano without knowing how," she said.

"Aw." He shuffled one foot as if trying to clear away a rock from the step.

"It's amazing."

He glanced at her, a smile in his eyes. "It was kinda sweet, sitting down and knowing how to play without being taught," he admitted.

"Not many people can do that, you know."

He shrugged, and she realized he was embarrassed. He'd probably received so little praise in his life, he wasn't sure how to act.

"I wish you had a piano," she told him.

He gave a little laugh. "Yeah, well, Granny wouldn't let me play it, if I did. She don't like music."

"Well, then, I wish we had one and you could use it."

He grinned at her. "I'd be over here more than I already am, I bet."

"That would be all right. Of course Mom would probably forbid you from playing if she was working in her studio."

"Yeah. Probably."

There was a short pause.

"Grown-ups," she sighed.

"Yeah."

Another short pause.

"E.Z.? Mr. Abernathy hasn't left yet."

"No foolin'?"

She shook her head. "And I don't know why."

E.Z. plucked at the frayed hem of his shorts. "Maybe he can't. Maybe you have to help him to, y'know, cross over. I saw it on this show one time. This woman talked to ghosts, and she'd tell 'em it's okay to go to the light. And they did."

"Oh, yeah? I've never done anything like that before. Besides, Janelle Dunmark finally left, and I didn't do anything to get rid of her. One day she just wasn't there, anymore."

Even in the dark, she could see an expression flit across E.Z.'s face. Then he looked down and pulled a thread free of his shorts. He said nothing, but she could tell he wanted to.

"What?" she asked.

He lifted one shoulder and kept rolling that thread between his thumb and his leg.

She nudged him gently with her elbow. "What's on your mind?"

"It's just that…well, who's this Janelle Dunmark you and your mom have mentioned? I'm not trying to be nosy, but I still want to know." He slid a glance sideways toward her. "If you don't mind telling me. You know I won't tell anyone else."

"I know that. And we're good enough friends I don't mind letting you know about her."

He turned toward her. "I'm listening."

She really didn't like thinking about or talking about Janelle. She hoped after this, she'd never have to mention the dead girl again, to anyone. It took a lot of grit to tell E.Z. what he was waiting to hear. Charlotte straightened her spine and took in a deep breath.

"One day, when I was six years old, I was in my room coloring. I kept hearing a tinkling sound, like wind chimes. It was like they were right in my room with me. And then, a little girl in a long dress and apron and a bonnet on her head was standing in my room. I never saw her come in or anything. She just stood there and looked at me."

E.Z.'s eyes got big. "Whoa."

"I thought she was another kid from our building. I asked her who she was, and she said, 'Janelle Dunmark.' She looked at my toys, so I told her she could play with them. I asked her questions, but she didn't say a word. When Mom came into the room, I asked her if Janelle lived in our building. She looked confused. I pointed right at Janelle, and it was like Mom couldn't see her, at all."

E.Z. shifted a little. "That's creepy."

"Mom told me I had a vivid imagination and walked out. I looked at Janelle and it seemed like she was going to cry, but she laughed instead. Now *that* was creepy."

"Yeah, man."

"Then she disappeared right in front of my eyes, like she was made of fog and a breeze had blown her away."

"Did you tell your mom?"

She crimped her mouth, remembering how confused and frightened she'd been.

"Yes. But she wouldn't believe me. She even told me it had been a dream." She huffed loudly. "E.Z., I knew that was no dream, but she insisted. From then on, Janelle would just show up."

"She didn't hang around, like Mr. A?"

"No. She was nothing like Mr. Abernathy. She threw my toys around. She broke stuff. Sometimes she'd go into the kitchen and open up the drawers. One time she unrolled all the toilet paper and paper towels in the house."

"No way!"

"Yes, way. And I'd get in trouble for it. Mom told me to stop talking about Janelle Dunmark and blaming my misbehavior on her. I told Mom it was the wind chimes that brought Janelle, but she really got upset about that. She took me to a head doctor, and I had to tell him everything. He told her I seemed to be all right, but maybe they shouldn't let me watch much television or read books. He also said I might need medication when I got older."

E. Z. clenched his fists. "That's lame! That's rotten. Didn't your dad say or do anything?"

"Dad was in the military then, so he wasn't home. But when he got back, he told me to let him know the next time Janelle was in the house."

E.Z. leaned forward eagerly. "And?"

"She made a terrible mess in my room. All my dolls' clothes had been taken off and scattered around. She'd ripped pages out of my coloring books, broken my crayons. Pulled the covers off the bed. Dad looked at that mess for a couple of minutes and asked if she was still there. I told him she was sitting in my little rocking chair. He put on that face he uses when he talks to people who're in trouble. I call it his 'cop face.' You know the one he gave us the other day?"

"Oh, yeah. That's a cold look. Froze my blood."

"Yeah. Well, he wore that expression. He looked right at that chair, just like he could see her and said, 'Janelle Dunmark, you've caused a lot of trouble that Charlotte's been blamed for. It's time for you to go away. Don't you ever come back, and I mean it."

He blinked. "Whoa. Do you think he could see her?"

"No, but she didn't come back very often, and never when Dad was home." She paused. "I wonder…."

"What?"

"Well, sometimes I wonder if I'll ever see her again."

"Do you want to?"

She shuddered. "No. She wasn't nice, and I think she's why my mom is afraid of my gift. If Janelle had been like Mr. Abernathy, helpless and in need, maybe Mom would have been sympathetic and understanding. Mr. Abernathy has never made messes or thrown anything around."

"That ghost kid was rotten."

"You got that right. I hope I *never* see more spirits like hers. They scare me." She shivered at the thought.

As if someone from beyond had been listening, a cool breeze blew across the porch, and with it came the sound of wind chimes, sweet and faraway. Charlotte's heart leaped. She reached out and grabbed E.Z.'s arm, hoping that by talking about Janelle Dunmark, she hadn't brought the girl's spirit back.

"Someone is coming," she whispered, peering into the night.

He turned and looked around. "Who? Where?"

"I don't know. Just wait." She scooted a little closer to him. The warm, solid strength of E.Z. near her made Charlotte feel better.

A soft glimmer of light in the front yard moved and shifted until it took the beautiful form of Great-Grandmum Ellen. Her smile was as lovely as before. Charlotte's heart filled with peace.

"Do you see someone?" E.Z. asked. He was still straining his eyes, peering into the dark in every direction.

"Yes," she whispered, afraid if she spoke aloud the

woman might disappear. "It's my great-grandmother. She came to me at my dad's."

"Where is she?" he whisper-shouted.

"She's coming toward us."

E.Z. tensed.

"Don't be afraid," Charlotte said softly. "She's really nice."

Ellen held out her hands as if she would gather them both to her, but her touch was merely a soft breath of air.

"Do you feel her here?" she said.

"I felt a cool breeze. Is that her? Is she scary?"

"Not at all. Beautiful and gentle. Like an angel."

"Whoa."

Ellen moved closer. "You're doing a good job, Charlotte, helping your mother cope with everything. And now, taking care of E.Z."

"Thank you, ma'am. We're good friends."

E.Z. snapped his head around to look at her in surprise. "Huh? Oh, you're talking to her, right?"

She nodded. "I'm talking about you, though."

He smiled. "Where is she?"

"Right in front of you, looking at you."

"Awesome." He faced the spirit directly, as if he could see her. "Charlotte is my best friend, ma'am. I think she's fantastic, and being able to see and talk to ghosts is, well, it's way awesome."

Ellen reached out and stroked the side of his face, her smile so sweet and loving that Charlotte, who hardly ever cried, felt tears sting her eyes.

"Whoa, Charlotte!" He grabbed her hand and held onto it so hard her fingers hurt. "Something … something … touched me."

"Great-Grandmum Ellen."

"Whoa, dude. Wow."

The spirit moved away a few steps. "This young man has a great future ahead of him. You and your father—and now your mother—are helping him to realize his worth."

"I'm so glad," Charlotte choked out. "And I'm glad Dad talked to Mom about E.Z."

"He did?" E.Z. said.

She nodded.

"Charlotte, you are so lucky to have such a great family," he said, smiling. "Even the ones who've, um, passed on."

Ellen's gentle laugh was like bells.

"I know," Charlotte said, smiling at him. "And now, you have us too."

He gave her hand one more squeeze and let go. "But what about Mr. A?"

"I don't know." She turned to her great-grandmother. "We found out how he died, and now he knows, but he's still here. Am I…" She swallowed hard. "Am I supposed to help him cross over? How do I do that?"

This time Ellen touched Charlotte's face. Cool and soft, like a kiss.

"Sweetheart, there have been spirits who've tried to

reach you and use you, like little Janelle. I was called on to intervene for you, and now I watch over you. This is why you've only sensed others, but never seen or contacted them. Now that you're growing up and reaching your potential, more will come to you. Some will reach out, others will merely stand by and watch. But never be afraid. I'll be near to guide and protect you."

"Thank you, Great-Grandmum. But what about Mr. Abernathy? He's the first spirit I've ever tried to help. I think I've failed."

"You haven't failed. Not at all. Clarence Albert Abernathy is not ready to move on. He must remain a while longer."

Charlotte's heart ached. "But he's waited so long already."

"Yes, but he has some things he must do first. And now he knows that. Remember, darling, he's never had anyone to help him before now."

"Then tell me what I'm supposed to do?"

Ellen smiled. "You'll know when the time comes."

"But—"

"You have known what to do for him up until now, haven't you? All that you need is here." Ellen's spirit hand touched Charlotte's chest, right over her heart. "And here." She touched her head. "Follow what you know is right."

"Oh, but—"

Her great-grandmother backed away, shimmering as

she left. "I'm watching over you. Be brave, be smart. Love your parents and your friends. Everything will be fine."

"But, Great-Grandmum, wait! Can't you tell me...?" Charlotte ran out into the yard, searching the shadows for a sign of her great-grandmother but everything looked normal. The only sound was crickets and tree frogs.

E.Z. joined her. He looked around as if he might spot the woman.

Charlotte fought against sorrow that tried to contain her. "She's gone."

"Oh. Where'd she go?"

"I don't know. She said she was always watching over me. I guess I won't see her very often."

E.Z. said nothing, as if he sensed Charlotte needed a few quiet moments. After a time, she drew in a deep breath. "Great-grandmum says Mr. A is not ready to leave yet. That I still need to help him." She swallowed the hard lump in her throat and blinked back her tears. "But I don't know what I'm supposed to do."

She looked at E.Z., and in the bluish glow of the streetlights, his hazel eyes were gentle and understanding. She saw his smile.

"Don't worry, Charlotte. You have me. Whatever needs to be done, we'll do it together."

"Promise?"

"One hundred percent. Promise!"

Hope filled her once more. After all, Charlotte

Franklin was not the kind of girl to give up or give in. Plus, how hard can it be to face the unknown when you have a best friend to help you?

"I think there are some cookies in the cookie jar." She smiled at him. "Want some?"

"Are you kiddin'? I'm starvin'!"

They ran back into the old yellow house together where Mr. Abernathy sat at the table, waiting for them. Charlotte would talk to him, comfort him, and help him move on when the time was right.

E.Z. went straight to the cookie jar and grabbed a couple of cookies. He handed one to Charlotte with a big grin, his eyes flashing with happiness.

She wondered what scary and crazy things might be ahead for a lonely boy, a gifted girl, and a displaced ghost. Life wouldn't be boring, that's for sure. One thing about it, though, she knew the three of them would be all right. After all, what could possibly be better than good friends you could count on?

~the end~

Not ready to say goodbye to Charlotte, Mr. Abernathy, and E.Z.? You can read the first chapter of the next book in the series – *Charlotte & Mr. Abernathy Shake the Family Tree.*

Also, feel free to download the Activity Guide from MotinaBooks.com.

Charlotte

&

Mr. Abernathy

Shake the

Family Tree

A weird sound woke Charlotte early Tuesday morning. Thump-spat thump-spat. What kind of racket was that? She'd been in a lovely dream about...about... what had she been dreaming about, anyway? That stupid thumpity-spat had chased it right out of her head.

She kicked off the top sheet, crawled out of bed, and slogged downstairs in her bare feet. At the foot of the steps, she paused and listened, then followed the sound to the front door.

E. Z. Bishop was sitting on the porch, throwing a small rubber ball against one of the posts and catching it. Thump-spat, thump-spat. She stared at him through the screen for a good five seconds then went outside in her pajamas and caught the ball the next time he tossed it.

"You're up." He didn't look the least bit annoyed that she had stopped his one-man game of catch.

"Yeah. Up before the sun," she grumbled.

In the last few weeks since she moved across the street from him in Park City, Arkansas, she'd gotten used to him showing up at odd times and in odd places. Tall and dark-haired, he was two years older than her, and cute in a scruffy sort of way. She liked him, but right then he annoyed her.

"What's the big idea?" she asked.

"About what?"

She held up the ball and scowled. "Thump-spat, thump-spat."

"Oh, that." He shrugged. "I didn't want to just sit here. I could've ridden my board, but the last time I did that before the sun was up, I nearly got creamed by a delivery truck."

One reason Charlotte liked E.Z. was that she could talk to him about anything, and he'd do his best to understand. There was no way he'd ever blab her secrets. Sometimes he shared his feelings and thoughts with her. Right then she could tell some-thing bothered him.

"Why do you always get up so early?" she asked.

"I like it. Besides, I couldn't sleep." He held out his hand for the ball, but she gripped it tightly and held it behind her. "I found that ball in the alley. Can I have it back?"

"In a minute. Why couldn't you sleep?"

He shrugged and stared across the street at his house. She sat down on the top step next to him and handed over the ball. It was unlike him to hold his thoughts in.

"Come on. Tell me." When he remained silent, she asked, "Your granny kick you out of the house again, didn't she?"

He shook his head. "Nah. She's asleep."

They sat, neither one speaking, as the sun edged upward and began to lay splashes of light along the landscape. Sooner or later, he'd tell her what was on his mind. She could wait.

"Look." E.Z. pointed to his house. "See how it looks like someone drew a silver line around our place? The sun does that, early in the morning." A few moments later, that sharp brightness softened, and edges blended with sunlight and shadow.

It was like him to see something cool about that ugly little house, to see something in a way no one else did.

"You hungry?"

He shrugged. Of course he was. E.Z. was always hungry.

She got to her feet. "I'll fix us some breakfast. Would you please bring in the newspaper for Mr. Abernathy?"

She started to turn away, but E.Z. stayed where he was, staring down at the ball in his hand. He examined it like he'd never seen a ball before.

"You hear me?"

"Yeah."

She studied his back, how sad he looked just sitting there. She sat beside him again. As early as it was, the day was already hot. The smell of baked earth and scorched grass mingled with the scent of whatever soap

E.Z. had used that morning.

"Tell me what's wrong."

"Nothin'."

"E.Z., you're my friend. Maybe I can help."

He remained silent.

Coaxing wasn't going to work, so she tried something else. "Tell me, or I'm going back in the house."

He blew out a deep breath. "It's my birthday Saturday."

"It is?" She gave him a big smile. "That's cool!"

He shook his head. "Not really."

"Of course it is, silly. Time to celebrate."

He glanced at her. "What's to celebrate? Fourteen years old, and I still don't know who my dad is."

Charlotte winced. It must be terrible not to know your own father.

"You don't even know his name?"

He shrugged again. "Evan Somebody. Or Somebody Evans. I dunno. I overheard Ma talking about him once to Granny, but they hushed when they saw me."

E.Z.'s mom was hardly ever around. His grandmother was grouchy and said hateful things. In fact, she made him stay out of the house most of the time. Neither of those women would probably even wish him a happy birthday, let alone have a party with cake and presents. Well, they might not celebrate his birthday, but she'd make sure he had a present or two and a cake with candles.

If she and her mom had lived in Park City long

enough to have made friends, they could have a party for him, but they'd only been here a few weeks. The only friends she'd made were E.Z., Shoji Tsuruoka at the library and, of course, Mr. Abernathy.

Mr. Abernathy was the ghost that lived in the kitchen of her house, and she was the only one who could see him. She got used to him pretty quick, and they'd had a lot of long chats in the last few weeks. Poor Mr. A had been in the kitchen since his death back in 1929. Every time he tried to leave the kitchen, he just…well, just faded away and ended up where he started. Charlotte had vowed to help him "move on" or "pass over" or whatever term anyone wanted to call it when a dead person finally left the earth. So far, he was still stuck in that kitchen, but thanks to Charlotte's investigations, at least he now knew how he'd died.

An idea stirred in the far corner of her brain. She coaxed it to life and thought about it until she realized it wasn't just a great idea—it was a fantastic idea.

"Hey, E.Z.?" she nudged him gently with her elbow, unable to keep the smile off her face.

"Huh?" He scraped his thumbnail over a place on the ball where something had gouged a small hole.

"You want to find your dad?"

He scoffed and said nothing, just kept scraping that hole like he thought he could fix it by rubbing it.

"Let's find your dad!"

His movements froze and he cut a glance at her sideways. "What d'ya mean?"

"What do you mean, what d'ya mean? Let's find your dad."

He turned to look at her full in the face, his expression bewildered. "We can't do that. We don't know where he is or who he is or nothing. He's probably in prison, even."

She tried not to be exasperated. "I thought you wanted to know about him."

"I do."

"Well, then…"

"What if he's in prison or dead or something?"

"I hope he isn't either of those things—"

"Me too!"

"—but if we do some investigating, we can find out." She paused and when he said nothing, did nothing, she leaned just a bit closer to him and added in a quiet voice, "At least you'd know."

He took in a deep breath, seeming to breathe in her words. A few seconds passed and then nodded. "You're right. I'd know and could stop guessing."

"Exactly."

"Exactly."

A few more silent seconds.

"So …?" she prodded.

A hesitation, then, "Okay, let's do it!" They grinned at each other as if they'd just found treasure. "When do we start?" he asked.

"Today. Right after breakfast. C'mon. You can help me make it." They got up. "What did you say your dad's name is? Evan?"

"That's part of it, but I don't know if it's his first or last name." E.Z. tossed the ball into the yard and they watched it roll to a stop.

The ringing of windchimes slipped through the morning air, not loudly, but insistently. Purposefully. That soft tinkling tone always signaled that a spirit was nearby, watching or reaching out to Charlotte. It was a sound she dreaded and usually tried to ignore. The presence of spirits often resulted in some kind of problem or need. Right then, E.Z.'s need was more important to her than whatever some dead person had in mind.

She paused at the doorway and ran a quick gaze along the porch and across the landscape. No one was out and about so early in the morning. Except…what was that movement over there?

She narrowed her eyes and tried to see if that was a little kid peeking at her from behind a tree across the street. She blinked, looked again. Sure enough, a small child peered out at her. Neither of his parents were nearby, and he was awfully young.

"Do you know that kid?" she asked E.Z.

"What kid?" He looked around, and she pointed across the street.

"That little kid over there close to your house."

E.Z. looked to where she pointed but shook his head. "I don't see him, but it might be Trevor. He lives down the street. Kinda early for him, though."

She stared hard. The child peeked at her again, then turned and darted away. The windchime rang loudly then fell silent.

Acknowledgements

Thanks to Diane Windsor and the staff at Motina Books who've been so kind and generous with their patience and help getting Charlotte ready for readers.

As always, thanks to my dearest best friend since childhood, Linda Knight, and my brother-at-heart, Gordon Bonnet, who read this book as a manuscript more than once.

Most especially, my enduring love, gratitude, and devotion goes to Brett Deiser whose belief in me never waivers.